KNIGHT EVENTS

By

Sheri Richey

Romance by Sheri Richey:

The Eden Hall Series:

Finding Eden

Saving Eden

Healing Eden

Protecting Eden

Completing Eden

∞

Willow Wood

Knight Events

A Small Town Christmas Anthology

Mystery by Sheri Richey:

Welcome to Spicetown

A Bell in the Garden

Spilling the Spice

Blue Collar Bluff

A Tough Nut to Crack

Chicory is Trickery

The No Dill Zone

CHAPTER ONE

It had been a beautiful drive from Ohio to Pennsylvania that morning. The cooling temperatures iced the bare winter branches until they sparkled. Gripping the steering wheel tightly, Jackie Knight reached to turn down the volume on her car radio. Nearing the city, the tranquility of the drive was replaced with the stress of traffic congestion and she took a deep breath. The disembodied female voice of her car navigation system, that she had nicknamed Stella, kept telling her that she had arrived at her destination, but it was obvious Stella had lost her groove.

"Where? Where is this place? I don't see anything that looks like a parking garage." As she turned right at the stoplight, the navigation system remapped her around the block again and she turned the radio off. Coasting into a bank parking lot, Jackie pulled her phone from her purse and called her friend, Calinda.

"Hey there," Calinda chirped. "I thought you were in Pittsburgh today."

"I am, but I'm lost. You've been here before, right? I keep going around in circles and Stella says I'm here. I'm not here. I'm nowhere!"

Calinda laughed. "You're driving around downtown, aren't you? You haven't seen it?"

"Oh, I know where the hotel is, but there's no place to put my car. The registration said there was parking. Where is it?"

"There are a couple of different garages downtown. You just have to find a place in one of them. I'm trying to remember--"

"Walk? Are you saying I have to walk blocks with my luggage? Are you kidding me?" Jackie threw her hands up in the air and slapped the steering wheel. "I've got heels on. I can't do that."

"Well, you could always drive to the airport and take the shuttle." Jackie frowned when Calinda laughed.

"Actually, that's not a bad idea."

"Oh, Jackie. You can handle this. It's not that far. Your suitcase rolls."

"That's not the point. Whatever happened to valet service? I'm being treated like a peasant!"

Calinda giggled. "Ah, the drama."

"You wish you were here, don't you?" Jackie smiled and took another cleansing breath. "This is stressing me out and I'm not even there yet."

"Why didn't you just sign up to participate by video? You said they offered that."

"Because I can't network on video. I wanted to meet these people. I'm trying to make big connections here. You don't understand the event planner world. I can't just spend my entire life being the Carlton, Ohio event planner. There's only so much to do in Carlton. These people are big time planners."

"So, you are thinking there is something more out there in the big wide world than what Carlton has to offer? If you remember, I tried that myself and came back home."

"I know. I know. You're boring." Jackie cackled with laughter. "I'm not trying to move to the city exactly. I just want to expand. I need to network and learn more about marketing. I want to grow into a company where I hire people to do events in neighboring towns and counties. Knight Events should be the go-to event planner for all of eastern Ohio. My business is just me in Carlton right now, but I've got bigger plans."

"Empire building!" Calinda teased. "Maybe you could take over the entire state. Why stop with just the east side?"

"I'm serious here! I'm trying to better myself and you're making fun of me. You've already got your dream business making wood stuff that rich people all over the country can't live without. I've just got Carlton. Small potatoes."

"No one would ever describe you as small potatoes, Jackie Knight."

"Oh, is that a jab at my size? I'm a big girl!" Jackie stood nearly six feet tall and carried herself proudly. Calinda was a wisp of a person, petite and delicate. They made quite the team.

Calinda laughed. "You know exactly what I'm talking about. You've got a big personality. It has nothing to do with your height."

Okay, let me try this again. If I never make it back, you know I ran out of gas in the vicinity of the Morrocan Hotel and I refused to walk."

"I've made a note," Calinda said solemnly.

"I'll call you later with an update on my progress, so you can live vicariously through me."

Jackie disconnected the call when she heard Calinda's laughter.

§

"Did you hear all that barking? He was going nuts out there!" Nolan Ramsey, Calinda's husband, stormed through the door and tossed a wet tennis ball on the padded window seat in his wife's wood turning workshop. Scuba, his hapless Otterhound, jumped up on the window seat to claim the ball after winning a quick game of fetch in the backyard.

"I didn't hear anything, but I was on the phone."

"He was a big joker, as usual. Slimed up the ball and wouldn't quit running around making loops in the yard, so I had to chase him to get the ball back. He can't even fetch like a normal dog."

Calinda smiled at Scuba, who was happily panting with his prize tennis ball between his large furry paws. "You were the one that just had to teach him a trick. Remember?"

"Yeah, I know." Nolan shrugged. "Who was on the phone?"

"Oh, just Jackie." Calinda blew on her worktable top and the wood shavings flew to the floor. "She's in Pittsburgh today for some training thing and she couldn't find parking."

"Training? They train you how to plan a party? I just thought it came naturally."

"It does to her. I wouldn't know the first thing about how to do it." Calinda flipped her protective mask down and repositioned the wood piece she was working on. "I'll probably hear from her a lot for the next couple of days. She doesn't know anyone at this conference, and she can't entertain herself very well. She'll need someone to talk to until she gets to know everyone."

Nolan started up the stairway but turned to lean on the hand railing. "Jackie makes friends pretty fast. I'm sure she'll be fine. Are you about ready for lunch?"

"Yeah, I'll be up as soon as I finish this side." Calinda flipped the switch on her exhaust fan as Scuba jumped off the window seat to follow Nolan upstairs. "Scuba is going to supervise, so make sure you don't drop any crumbs."

§

Jackie heaved a sigh of defeat as she rounded the corner of the hotel, dragging her rolling suitcase. Her shoulders sagged when she looked up at the grand front entrance several feet above the city street and atop a full staircase. For a moment, she considered her options. She could just turn and go back to her car. She could be home in a couple of hours. The money she spent for the conference was lost, whether she made it up those steps or not. At this point, she didn't care if she went. She was tired, frustrated and perspiring in all the wrong places. She couldn't let anyone see her like this.

"Can I help you with that?"

Jackie gasped, startled that someone had approached from behind without her hearing them, and glanced suspiciously over her shoulder. A short middle-aged man with round glasses smiled at Jackie.

"Are you checking in? Can I carry your bag?"

Accepting that fate had made the decision for her, she smiled.   "That would be wonderful. I would really appreciate it."

"No problem.   The parking here is horrible."

"I know," Jackie said, dabbing her hand across her forehead. Although her nose must be bright red from the chilly wind, she had heated up from the walk. "I had no idea there was no valet service." Pulling herself up the stairs by the handrail, her shoes clicked on the steps as she scurried to keep up with her suitcase. "Let me get the door."

"Are you here for the conference? The event coordinator training?"

"Yes! You, too?" Jackie followed him through the double doors into the lobby and took a deep breath as she grabbed the handle of her rolling bag.

"Yeah. I'm Mitchell Todd, by the way."

Jackie reached out to shake Mitchell's offered hand. "I'm Jackie. Jackie Knight. I have a small business in Carlton, Ohio, called Knight Events."

"Nice to meet you, Jackie. I work for the company that's hosting the conference, Mackey Enterprises. I tried to tell my boss that the parking was an issue, but he wanted to hold it here. The meeting rooms are nice, though."

"I'm sure they are and thank you so much, Mitchell. I really appreciate your help."

"Please call me Mitch. You're very welcome. Just go right up there and check in. After you get settled, come down to the registration tables over here on the left," Mitchell said, pointing down the hallway.

"Is there time for lunch? I didn't get a chance to eat."

"Maybe not, but there will be snacks and drinks in the conference room. I might be able to rustle you up a sandwich."

"Thank you again. I'm so glad I ran into you. Are you doing the trainings?"

"Oh, no. My boss, Erik, does all the training. I'm just the coordinator of the event coordinator." Mitchell chuckled at his own joke. "I do all the work and Erik gets all the credit."

"I'm sure he appreciates you." Jackie smiled and shifted her weight to drop her purse on the counter. That was what she needed, someone to coordinate her.

Mitchell shrugged his shoulders and pointed as a hotel clerk waited to catch Jackie's attention. "I'll see you inside."

CHAPTER TWO

"Mitch! Where's the extra copy of Pamela's notes? I left my copy in my room." Erik Mackey dropped a stack of programs on the registration table. "If you don't have one, run upstairs and get my folder. Did you confirm with the hotel that they'd bring the snacks early? Remember, no peanuts. We want fresh fruit." Erik turned his back on Mitch without waiting for a response and welcomed two young women who walked up to the registration table. Mitch knew what he needed to do.

"Hi, again." Jackie wiggled her fingers at Mitch as she walked up to the registration table.

"You found us." Mitch smiled and looked over at Erik. "You just need to sign in here and grab your name badge. The room is right behind me."

Jackie walked into the banquet room and found an empty table. Many were filled already with participants chatting noisily with each other or on their phones. Jackie took the opportunity to check her phone messages and her email. She was planning the annual Carlton Chamber Christmas dance now, and there were still details to work out. It wasn't really the best time for her to be away, and she had no one else to take care of things when she wasn't there.

Jackie had been planning all the parties in Carlton, Ohio, for over ten years and it dictated her life. Sure, there were lulls and free time, but it was always in between holidays or during terrible weather. She wanted the chance to have a life that allowed her the freedom to take a vacation when she chose or celebrate Christmas in Paris, if the opportunity arose. She wanted to delegate, supervise, and oversee. She was tired of doing everything herself, but her income just didn't allow her to hire regular staff and her income wasn't growing.

"Here you go, Jackie." Mitch walked in front of the table and placed a white binder in front of her. "This has the daily programs listed and notes on all the trainings that we cover. There's even room in the back for you to make your own notes. I forgot to give you one when you signed in."

"Thank you."

"Care if I sit a minute?" Mitch pulled the chair from the table in front of Jackie's and sat facing her with his hands clasped on the table. "I talked to the wait staff and they said they would sneak you in a little something to eat. Oh, here they are now." Mitch waved his hand in the air and a young woman handed him a small plate with a sandwich and a bottle of water.

"Thank you." Jackie smiled at the hotel attendant. "I really appreciate it."

"I'm not sure what that is." Mitch peered at the plate. "Maybe chicken salad?"

Jackie took a bite and nodded her head in agreement.

"Anyway, I'd love to hear more about your business. You said it was in Ohio? How far was your drive today?"

Jackie glanced down at Mitch's hands and saw a wedding band. He was behaving like a nervous high school boy who was learning how to flirt. Surely, he wasn't hitting on her.

"Just a couple of hours," Jackie said after swallowing. "Carlton is in eastern Ohio."

"Hmm, I don't recognize the name, but me and the wife, we drive through Ohio a couple of times a year. I thought maybe it was a town we passed through. Her mom lives down in southern Ohio and we go visit pretty often."

"You live here in Pittsburgh?" Jackie dabbed a napkin across her mouth and eyed her sandwich again.

"Yeah, but not in the city. We're out in the burbs," Mitch said with a chuckle. "Kids are all grown and gone now. Me and the missus are always talking about moving. She wants to move closer to her mom, but I'd like to go a little further south. Knowing us, we'll talk it to death and never do it."

Jackie nodded as she chewed.

"You have any kids, Jackie?"

Jackie shook her head, no, and held up a finger to finish chewing. She just wanted to finish eating before the training started. "Sorry, no. No children. You?"

"Yeah, we've got two boys. One is just about done with college and the older one is working in Maryland now. Sure as we move away, we'll have grandkids and my wife will make us move back!" Mitch turned sideways in his chair and laughed.

Jackie brushed the crumbs from her fingers and took a drink of water. "So, tell me about Mackey Enterprises."

Mitch turned back in his chair to face Jackie. "It's a good company. I used to have a small company of my own, like you do. Erik's dad actually picked me up and I took over events in the northern suburbs for Mackey Enterprises. Erik is the boss now. His dad retired a few years back." Mitch glanced at the door and nodded his head. "That's Erik that just walked in."

"Oh, it must be about time to start." Jackie looked around the room for a place to throw away her plate.

"Yeah, I better sneak out while I can. We'll meet up for dinner tonight and all go out somewhere together." Mitch stood and returned the chair to the other table. "The first night we always offer a group dinner since most people aren't familiar with the area. Erik will tell you about it at the end of training. I'll see you later."

"Thanks so much, Mitch, for lunch and for all your help today."

Mitch just nodded and smiled as he walked toward the double doors in the back of the room.

§

Nolan Ramsey held the door to The Villa open for Calinda to walk through. She had placed a wood order at the hardware store, and they had decided to have dinner in town. The Villa was Carlton's finest and Nolan was hungry.

"Hi! Will there just be the two of you?" A young girl with a ponytail bounced up and down on her toes as she pulled out laminated menus from the stand near the door.

Nolan nodded to the hostess as Calinda looked first to the left and then the right. Frowning when she heard the high-pitched squeal of a small child come from the dining room, she pointed toward the bar. "We'd like a booth in the bar, please."

"Sure! Follow me."

Before sliding into the booth, Calinda glanced at the bar and motioned to Nolan with a tilt of her head. "Larry Stanley is over there."

"Do you want me to go over and invite him to join us?"

Calinda looked over her shoulder. "I don't think that's a good idea."

"Why not?"

"It looks like he's trying to flirt with Laura." Calinda rolled her eyes.

"Nah. He's not interested in Laura Madison." Nolan scooted sideways to leave the booth, but Calinda clamped her hand over his.

"No," Calinda whispered as Nolan gave her a questioning look. "Jackie would kill me and I just don't want--"

"Are you kidding me? Why would Jackie care if Larry joined us for dinner? He's still our friend." Nolan leaned back in his seat and squared his shoulders. "She can hate him if she wants, but that's not changing anything for me."

"Oh, she doesn't hate him. It would just seem disloyal." Calinda shrugged. She couldn't explain it to him, but she knew Jackie, and Jackie would be hurt if they invited Larry to dinner, even though they just ran into him by accident. The town would carry the story that the three of them had dinner together and Jackie would hear about it.

"Nonsense," Nolan huffed as a waitress approached to ask for their order.

"Did you see our specials tonight?" The waitress pointed to the chalk board on the wall.

Calinda smiled and gave the young girl her order. When the waitress stepped closer to Nolan for his order, Calinda stole a quick peek at the bar. Laura Madison was the usual bartender during the week. She had gone to school with Calinda and Jackie. Larry had one leg on the barstool and the other on the floor. As Nolan finished up his order, Calinda chanced another glance only to see what was in the chair next to Larry.

"I'll bring your drinks right out." The waitress took their menus as she walked away.

"Nolan, what's in the chair beside Larry?"

Nolan glanced back to the bar and squinted. "It looks like crutches. Yeah, there's something wrong with his foot." Nolan pointed to the bar. "Hey, Larry."

Calinda closed her eyes and shook her head.

Nolan waved when Larry turned around, and Larry returned the wave. "Maybe he'll hobble over here before he leaves. It looks like he's wearing some kind of cast. I haven't seen him in several weeks."

"Here you go," the waitress said as she placed drinks on the table. "Your food will be right up."

"Thank you," Calinda said to the waitress as she folded a napkin to put under her drink. "Stuff happens, honey. He must have hurt himself, or maybe he just had surgery of some sort."

"Or maybe he was in a dangerous foot chase with a perp." Nolan tossed his head back in laughter and Calinda smirked.

"That's very possible. Carlton does have crime, you know. I'm sure he's had to chase people before."

"I guess." Nolan shrugged. "I like Larry, but all I ever see him do is drive around town in a squad car. He looks like he has it pretty easy."

"He's over the other patrolmen. He's a lieutenant, so he has to keep an eye on them. Jackie always said they call him for every little thing, and he tells them what to do or he goes to help them. She found it rather annoying when they dated, I think, but he does do a lot of stuff."

"Here he comes," Nolan said, smiling. "Hey buddy, you got lead in that boot?"

"Feels like it," Larry said as he lifted his foot. "It could come in handy if I run across anybody that needs a good kick though. What are you two up to tonight?"

"Ah, just getting a bite to eat. Wanna join us?"

"Thank you, but I'm on my way to my mom's house. She's expecting me for dinner tonight. My little brother, Greg, is home visiting this week. You know Greg, don't you, Calinda?"

"Yes, Greg was a year ahead of me in school. Where does he live now?"

"He's been in Indiana for the last couple of years, but he moves around a lot with his job. He's getting divorced and I think he's hiding out in Carlton." Larry chuckled. "At least that's what I told him it looks like to me. My mom's happy to see him, though."

"I'm sure she is." Calinda smiled. Jackie must not know about Greg's visit or she would have mentioned it to her. She loved having stories before Jackie got them. It happened so seldom, but now Calinda wondered whether it was a good idea to tell her.

"See you guys later." Larry moved quickly through the tables to the door. This was clearly not his first time navigating on crutches.

Nolan hummed as he frowned at Calinda. "We still don't know what happened to his foot. Larry's a secretive guy."

Calinda grinned. "The reason you don't know is because you didn't ask. Women ask direct questions and get facts. Guys chum around and find out nothing. Sometimes I don't know how any of you get through life."

"Well..." Nolan gave a helpless shrug and laughed. "Women tell us!"

"Oh, go ask Laura. I'm sure she asked him." Calinda tilted her head toward the bar and Nolan scooted out of the booth.

CHAPTER THREE

Jackie sat on the couch in the lobby of the hotel with other conference attendees as Mitch gathered everyone around. The group was headed to a Mexican restaurant just one block from the hotel and he had reserved a large room there so they could all sit together. A light snow was falling, but Jackie was relieved the forecast didn't warn of any significant snowfall. She wanted to wear her dress boots, not her frumpy snow boots, and she did have to drive back home in a few days.

"Okay, guys." Mitch motioned for everyone to stand. "Let's head out. Stick together. I don't want to lose anyone."

Jackie had no one to stick with, so she tried to blend. It seemed that most of the participants were from larger firms, or they knew others in the group already. She always had more difficulty fitting in with large groups of women. Men she could handle.

"Good evening," Erik Mackey said as he offered Jackie his arm. "I don't think we've formally met, but I saw you in class today."

Jackie smiled and accepted his arm. She was pleased to see that even with her boots on, she didn't have to look down at him. "I'm Jackie."

"Well, Jackie. What do you say? Are you up for some Mexican food? It's really very good. Once I found this place, I started bringing all of my training classes here and I try to stop in anytime I'm downtown."

"Do you live here in the city? You do events in this area?"

"Oh, I run all over this city. We love having events in the downtown area, especially at Christmas time. The city lights are beautiful. I don't really get involved much at the ground floor planning level anymore with individual events."

"That's what I'm hoping to do someday. I'd like to have lots of events going on all at once, all over the place." Jackie waved her arms.

"Are you wanting to move to the city?"

"Oh, no. I'd like to expand in my area of Ohio. I think there are a lot of towns near me that don't have anyone." Jackie shivered and wrapped her scarf closer around her neck as they walked into the wind.

"Ah, I'm sure the conference will offer you lots of information to help with that. We have a session on franchising and personnel management. Both of those will be something you'll need to consider for the future."

"That's great," Jackie said as she looked across the street at the businesses with lighted Christmas windows. "Hiring people is something I need to do. I just don't know how to find the right person. I hire people now just for a specific job at an event. I need a regular assistant full time that I can count on every day. I don't know who that person could be. I just haven't found anyone yet." That was true. At least that was part of the problem. Jackie hadn't found anyone in

Carlton who had the flare she did with decorating and organizing events. She needed to look outside of Carlton, but even if she found the right person, how would she afford to pay them?

"You know, I wouldn't suggest this to just anyone, but there is something that might work well in your situation." Erik held the door to the restaurant open so Jackie could walk in first. "If you could find another event planner somewhere in your area, the two of you could merge. Then you'd have a partner that was already trained and capable, plus they'd have their own connections and events planned so the financial burden isn't there. Have you thought of that before?"

Jackie took a deep breath and frowned. She wanted to be in charge. She didn't want a partner. "As far as I know, I'm the only event planner in eastern Ohio, but I do see the benefits. It's just not really the direction I'd like to go."

"Just a thought," Erik said, smiling. "We'll figure it out."

"So, what do think?" Pamela sat on the edge of the bed and pulled off her shoe. Massaging her foot, she glanced up at Erik. "You spent a lot of time chatting up the tall girl with black hair. Is she a favorite?"

Erik smiled as he unbuttoned his shirt. "Yeah, I think old Mitch came through for us this time. That was Jacqueline Knight. She has a single-owner business in some tiny nowhere town in Ohio. She seems pretty eager."

"Yeah? Is she willing to stay put? We don't need another one who wants to move to the big city." Pamela switched her focus to her other foot. "Mitch can be a little naïve at times."

"I'm not sure yet, but it looks good. I'm going to ask her to dinner tomorrow night, just the two of us. I'll have to see how it goes."

"Anybody else catch your eye?" Pamela frowned. "I can't remember the name, but there was a young woman that got here really early today. She was wearing a red dress and had short brown hair. Did you see her? I thought she was interesting, but I got interrupted. I'm going to try talking to her again tomorrow. She might be an option."

"Was her name Amy?" Erik tossed his shirt on the bed.

"That sounds right. I think she lives north of here. I can't remember the name of the town."

"If she's the one I'm thinking of, she's financed by family. I don't think she'll be a sound choice. Maybe in a few years, but she's too young right now. I'm going to take a shower."

Pamela nodded and slipped her phone from her pocket as Erik closed the bathroom door. She wished she could trust Erik's instincts, but she couldn't.

§

"Good morning! Is it too early?"

"Not for me. I'm always in the shop before eight o'clock," Calinda said as she slipped on her apron. "You are the one that's never up this early."

Jackie dabbed a small eyeshadow brush into a tiny pot of glimmering taupe and blew on the brush. "Don't I know it! It's sinful, but these folks want to start the training early, so I've only got a few minutes. You won't believe what happened last night."

"What happened?"

"I went out for dinner last night with a big group of people from the conference. The main guy, the guy that owns the company, he sat with me. His name is Erik and he is amazing. I told him all about the Christmas dance and he said he wants to see Carlton."

"Why?"

"Because he's captivated by me! Why do you think?" Jackie cackled with glee. "The rest of these ladies are boring. Not only is he hot, but he has all kinds of ideas about how I can grow my business. He's running a huge company with a bunch of event planners. He knows every angle. He walked me to my door last night after dinner and kissed my hand. Isn't that gallant?"

"So, is this a professional interest or a love interest?" Calinda put her phone on speaker and began picking through a box of small wood pieces. "I'm not sure I'm following."

"That's the beauty of it," Jackie screeched. "He can be both! I need a date to the dance, and I need someone to help me expand my business. Erik is all that and more."

"This guy lives in Pittsburgh?" Calinda was suspicious. "He runs a company there and he wants to come to Carlton?"

"Not to live here. He just wants to see it. He wants to see what it's like and then he can give me some suggestions to grow. He's full of big ideas. He's a fascinating guy."

"Hmm, okay. You'll definitely shake the town up when you show up with a new guy."

"I know," Jackie said with a low growl. "And I love that part."

Calinda couldn't hold in her laughter. Jackie's theatrics were her most endearing quality and she never tired of Jackie's ability to entertain.

"I've got to get downstairs so I can grab some breakfast before it starts."

"Are the classes any good?"

"Eh, they're okay. I'm not really hearing anything I didn't already know," Jackie said. "The benefits are in the networking. I'm meeting lots of other people doing what I do and hearing about some of their events, so it gives me new ideas. Maybe I'll try setting up karaoke at the Stanley Christmas party this year. A lady from Virginia says it's been a big hit with her family reunions. People aren't as shy around their own family."

"That could work."

"Gotta go. Talk to you soon."

"Okay, bye," Calinda said, knowing Jackie was already off the line. Jackie didn't like to say goodbye.

CHAPTER FOUR

"Nolan, where are you?" Calinda was relieved when he answered the phone. She wanted him home now. "Something is happening out here!"

"I'm just turning down Willow Wood Road now. I'm almost there. What's happening?"

"Fire trucks keep going by and I smell something burning. I don't know what it is, and I can't find Scuba. I keep calling for him and he doesn't come. We need to find out--"

"Okay. Okay, I'll drive down past the house and see if I can see where the trucks went. You keep yelling for Scuba. Try that dog whistle. It might work."

"It smells like it's really close. We may have to evacuate. There was a fire risk advisory out because it has been so dry. I hope it's not someone's home."

"Scuba is usually home in the late afternoon. I hope he's not in the middle of this somehow. I don't think he has enough sense to run from a fire."

"Hurry home." Calinda hated that pleading sound in her voice, but after one year of marriage, she felt lost without Nolan at her side. She began opening drawers in the workshop to search for the dog whistle. She and Nolan both needed Scuba home and it was the only way she knew to help.

Finding the whistle and grabbing a bag of dog biscuits, Calinda ran outside into the backyard. "Scuba! Scuba! I've got treats!" Shaking the bag and blowing the whistle, she ran back by the pond to repeat her pleas. "Treats! I've got treats! Scuba!"

Just as she turned to walk to the other side, Scuba came bounding out of the woods from the direction of Nolan's house and ran around the side of the pond. Before they married, Nolan had lived just on the other side of the woods from her and he had that house up for sale now. She knew Scuba returned to the house from time to time to check on things. He hadn't forgotten it was his home once.

"Oh, you silly boy. You had me worried to death." Calinda stuffed treats in his mouth and started jogging back toward the house, knowing Scuba would follow along. As she reached the back door, her cell phone rang.

"I found him!" Calinda looked down at Scuba and whispered, "It's your daddy."

"You found Scuba? Thank goodness. The fire got the Parker's house. They are trying to put it out now, but the house is gone. I'm going to help Tom get his hunting dogs out of the cages in the back of his property and move them down to the Hodge's Farm. They said they could board the dogs there."

"Are his dogs okay?"

"Yeah, the fire didn't get back there, but they can't stay here alone. Can you call the police station and ask them to help find Tom and Betty's son?   Betty said he should be down at the drugstore picking up her prescription or at the hardware store. He went to run some errands for them and he's not answering his phone."

"Sure, I'll call. You can bring Tom and Betty down to our house. We've got plenty of room and they can stay here as long as they need." Calinda climbed the stairs from her workshop in the back of the house to the main living area and let Scuba inside.

"Maybe tonight, but I think I'm going to offer my house to them. It's just sitting over there empty and there's no reason they can't stay there as long as they need."

"That's a great idea. I'll put some coffee on. Hurry home!"

§

"I'm glad you were free to join me tonight, Jackie. I've been looking forward to some uninterrupted time for us to talk. I really want to hear more about you and Carlton, Ohio." Erik pulled out a chair for Jackie and walked around the small round table to face her. "The food here is exquisite. Would you permit me to order for you?"

Jackie glanced briefly at a wine list on the table and assumed she would also be unable to read the menu. "I'd be delighted."

As the waiter approached, Jackie looked around the room and at the adjacent tables. Assuming Erik was speaking French, Jackie became concerned whether she was brave enough to eat such unfamiliar food. Hopefully, the hotel could make her another sandwich when she returned.

"You look lovely tonight," Erik said as the waiter was dismissed. "If I neglected to say that earlier, I apologize."

Jackie smiled nervously. "This is a lovely place. It must be nice to have a variety of places to eat. My small town has very limited options."

"Oh, I only come here for special occasions. Honestly, I don't dine out that often. I enjoy cooking. If I hadn't gone into my father's business, I probably would have gone to culinary school."

"Really!" Jackie leaned back in her seat. A man that cooked was truly a special find for her. "That's fascinating."

"Do you cook?"

"Not a thing." Jackie laughed loudly at his bewildered expression and scrunched up her shoulders when she realized other patrons were staring. "Sorry, I know I'm too loud. I'll try to behave."

"No," Erik said as he reached for her hand. "Your laugh is one of the things that draws me to you. You are bubbling with excitement, and that's the very best way to live life."

Jackie shrugged her shoulders. "It's just me. I can't help it."

"But I would guess party planning comes naturally to you as well. You enjoy what you do?"

"I do, but I didn't really plan to be an event coordinator. I went to college and got a business marketing degree. My vision was advertising, but along the way, I planned a lot of parties." More cautious now, she covered her mouth to quiet her laughter. "There really wasn't anyone else in town to do it. We needed to have events and no one else stepped up to make them happen, so the business just fell in my lap."

"So how did you hear about our conference?"

Jackie started to speak but paused when the waiter arrived to open the wine. Erik sniffed and he swirled before sniffing again. Once he finally approved of the wine, Jackie took a tiny sip and grimaced. Luckily, Erik had not seen the scowl, and Jackie reminded herself of her pledge to behave.

"You were about to tell me how you learned about our conference."

"Oh, yes. Well, I enrolled from an online ad I saw. I've always wanted to take the time to network with other event coordinators and share experiences. When you are the only game in town, as I am, you don't have anyone to talk to about such things. I'd like to grow my business, but I can't clone myself to be in three places at once."

"One of the topics tomorrow is how to hire staff and expand. You're in an excellent position to do just that! I'm sure that Mackey Enterprises can help you. My father started this company as a one-man show many moons ago, and now we have a dozen events going on simultaneously. Recently, we've even begun European tours. I just came back from Spain where I negotiated with the locals for an event we are coordinating. You know, destination events are all the rage now."

"No," Jackie said with a muffled chuckle. "I didn't know. I don't think that news has reached Carlton yet. Most of the people there have never given a thought to leaving Ohio."

"I wouldn't suggest you consider that avenue, of course. City folks and country folks have different goals in mind, no doubt. I'm just using that as an example. You never stop growing or trying new things. Mackey Enterprises is still exploring new levels to reach, and you should be doing the same. It's the nature of our business - exceeding our customers' expectations."

"I'm just helping those *country folks* get together and have a good time." Jackie managed her facial muscles successfully and was able to say that without a sneer. "Most of my events center around family or town celebrations."

"What do you have going on right now?"

"Oh," Jackie squirmed to sit higher in her seat. "It's always a busy time for me around the holidays. I have the Chamber's Christmas dance on my shoulders right now.

It's just a little more than a week away, and right after that I have the Stanley family Christmas celebration. It's a big family reunion. I hardly get a breath before it's the new year and Christmas is crazy for everyone, I'm sure."

Erik hummed as Jackie followed his gaze to the approaching waiter. The food had arrived. It took Jackie only moments to determine the food was no more tolerable than the wine and she was going to need that sandwich later. The vegetable was the only thing she trusted, and she proceeded to move that around her plate.

"So, what exactly is involved in the dance you mentioned?"

"It's an annual event. It used to be just a dinner party for the members. We expanded it to a vendor sale during the day and an open party for the town in the evening. Now everyone in town comes and it's a big event. All the chamber members set up booths to show their products or services during the day. Then at night, we have the dance and a silent auction to fund next year's event. It's really great fun once all the work is done. Everyone gets together in their finest attire and we can get about two hundred people in the school gym, so it's packed."

"This is held at a school?"

"Well, we just use the high school gym because it's the biggest facility we have. It's not connected to the school in any way, but it's easy to turn into a ballroom and we have a stage for the band. We have another similar dance in the fall. My town does like to party if it pays for itself."

"You just have the one high school in town?" Erik nodded as if he already knew the answer.

"Yes, just one high school. The kids actually enjoy helping with the decorations and I never turn down free help." Jackie smiled and took a big drink of water.

"Is everything okay with your meal? It doesn't look like you've even tried your Blanquette de Veau."

"Oh, no. It's fine. It's good. I'm just tired. Not much appetite tonight." Jackie dabbed the white cloth napkin across her lips. The white lumpy meat dish in front of her had an unusual texture, but she stabbed a mushroom floating in the white sauce and popped it in her mouth. She pushed the meat to one side of her plate hoping to make it appear she had eaten half of it.

"Enough shop talk," Erik said as he pushed his plate to the side. Jackie promptly tossed her napkin over her uneaten meal and followed Erik's lead. "I want to hear about you. I assume you are not married since you agreed to have dinner with me, but have you ever been married or have any children?"

"No, I'm not married." Jackie lifted her water glass again and took a sip. "No children."

"Working in the entertainment business doesn't leave much time for that sort of thing." Erik leaned back from the table and smiled. "Do you ever think of it that way? That we are in the entertainment business?"

"Certainly," Jackie said, nonchalantly. "I do try my very best not to <u>be</u> the entertainment, but I definitely agree that I work in that business."

Erik chuckled. "So, do you have a date for your Christmas dance?"

"No, but I'm usually running around all evening among friends. I have a good time once the work is done."

"Well, unless you think I will be a bother, I'd like to see your quaint little town and attend your dance. Do you think that would be okay?"

Jackie hesitated a moment. This seemed too good to be true. "Of course, that would be okay. Carlton would love to have a new face at the party."

"Great! I bet you can introduce me to every one of those two hundred people, too. Can't you?" Erik's smile was engaging, and Jackie hoped he wasn't mocking her town.

"I probably can," Jackie said, nodding. *And I'll make sure everyone there knows you are my date.*

CHAPTER FIVE

"You'll never believe what I'm about to tell you." Jackie hit the speaker button on her phone so she could free her hands.

"What? It must be good," Calinda said. "I can hear you smiling."

"I have a date to the Chamber Christmas dance with a handsome, sophisticated city boy. He formally committed last night. He had mentioned it and hinted about it the other evening, but I wasn't certain he would really come."

"Oh, that'll make Larry jealous."

"Larry? I'm not trying to make Larry jealous. He wouldn't care anyway. I'm talking about Erik. He asked me if he could come. He wants to see Carlton and go to the dance. Can you believe that?"

"So, the dinner was more a date than a casual bite to eat?"

"Yes, and I was not prepared for that. We went to some swanky French place. He had to order because the menu wasn't in English and I couldn't eat a bit of it. I don't even know what it was, but he did all that because he wants to see me after the conference. I didn't expect that."

"You had to know he was interested. He asked just you to dinner and he has a whole class of people that probably wanted to go to dinner with him."

"Maybe, but he started out just talking about work stuff and I thought maybe he had picked me because I was there alone, and a lot of the others came in groups of friends or work associates. I wasn't even sure it was going to be just us. He has employees around him during the day. I thought maybe that guy, Mitch, might join us. I didn't know for sure."

"If he invited himself to the Christmas dance, he definitely wants to see you. No one just wants to go to a Christmas dance."

"Now I can hear your eyes rolling." Jackie laughed. "I didn't realize he was really into me. Maybe my radar is off."

"Maybe being out of town with unfamiliar people has gotten you off your game."

"Hmm." Jackie leaned toward the bathroom mirror to stroke on her blush.

"Speaking of Larry, we saw him last night."

"Who was speaking of Larry?" Jackie snapped. "I haven't seen him in months. Despite the small town, he has managed to stay out of my path for quite a while now."

"Well, he's hurt. He's on crutches, but I don't know the story behind it. Nolan asked Laura Madison if she knew and she said he dodged the question when she asked him. I thought maybe you'd heard something."

"No. Everyone knows better than to talk to me about Larry. Everyone but you!" Jackie sprayed some perfume behind each ear. "You'll like Erik. He's smart and very tall. You know I don't like short men."

Calinda giggled. "Yes, I know, but doesn't he live in Pittsburgh? Are you going to start having a long-distance relationship? Or is he going to talk you into the city?"

"Oh, I'm not ever moving to Pittsburgh. I wouldn't say I'll never leave Carlton. I might someday, but I don't have any interest in living in the city."

"But this Erik has a business, right? He's not going to consider leaving that. What would he do in Carlton? We already have an event planner!"

"True, but you're getting ahead of me. I just called to tell you I have a date for the dance. Let's just stick to that for right now."

"Okay," Calinda said. "So, what are you going to wear?"

"Oh no. I don't have any idea. Maybe I need a new dress. I might need to go shopping before I come home. What's my best color? Red? Maybe that's too bright. Royal blue? Why don't you drive over in the morning and go shopping with me? We're done at ten o'clock. I can check out of the hotel and we'll hit the stores." Jackie layered gold and silver bracelets on her left wrist and slipped on her rings.

"I don't need a new dress. I'm not going to that dance."

"You aren't even going to meet Erik? He's just coming for the dance and I'm sure he'll go back the next morning. You and Nolan could come and then I'd have someone to leave him with if I get called away for a sound problem or catering issue. You're my wing man!"

"I have no wings. You know I hate these events--"

"But you and Nolan can reminisce about how you met. It will be romantic. Maybe Erik and I will follow the same path. Maybe we'll make out in the parking lot for hours." Jackie cackled with laughter, picturing Calinda scowling despite the blush of embarrassment.

"I'm going to ignore that since I can't smack you through the phone."

"I know. I know. You don't want to talk about that, but I think it's sweet." Jackie slipped on her shoes and took one last long look in the mirror. Red was a good color on her.

"So, what's on the schedule for tonight? It's your last night in the big city. Are you going out again?"

"I don't know. I'm playing it by ear."

"Okay. I'll see you tomorrow. Drive safe."

§

The next morning Jackie leaned on the registration counter at the hotel front desk and tried to look around the corner for a desk clerk. Still huffing and puffing from her walk back to the hotel from the parking garage, she blew out air to flutter her bangs and slumped against the counter. The concierge desk was not occupied, and the front desk staff were busy. She had already checked out and just wanted to go home.

"Hey, Jackie. Are you checking out?" Mitch dropped a small overnight bag at his feet.

"I checked out earlier, but when I went to my car, I have a flat tire." Jackie rolled her eyes. She had dropped her towing coverage on her insurance years ago because she rarely left town. In Carlton there were a number of people she could call to come help her, but here, she didn't know where to begin. It had to happen the one time all year that she left town.

"Oh, no. I'm sure we can call someone." Mitch walked to the other end of the counter and peered through the side door. "Someone will show up here any minute and they'll know who to call. Or maybe Erik knows someone." Mitch pulled out his cell phone to text Erik.

"There's probably a garage nearby." Jackie glanced at the time. She had told Mrs. Stanley that she would drop by this evening to go over her menu plan, but she knew she could always reschedule that for another evening.

"Can I help you?" A young girl in a red vest and Moroccan Hotel name tag clasped her hands on the counter.

"Oh, yes. I just checked out a few minutes ago, but my car has a flat tire. Is there someone local you can call to help me?"

"Uh, let me ask. Just a second..."

"What's going on?" Erik bounced up to the front desk in jeans and a closely fitted knit shirt. Jackie had only seen him in suits all week, but this gave her the opportunity to admire his physique. He must have a gym visit scheduled every day to maintain that look.

"The lady at the front desk is checking," Mitch said. "Do you know anyone around downtown that Jackie could call to come change her tire?"

Before Erik could reply, the front desk clerk returned. "I'm going to do an online search and print it for you so you can decide who you want to call. There are several options in the area."

"I've got an auto service that does that stuff for me. I don't really know anybody to call directly." Erik rubbed his chin. "Do you have a spare in your trunk?"

"Yes, I think so. I mean I should have." Jackie brightened in the hope Erik could just change her tire and she could be on her way.

"Oh, good. That always makes it easier, I think. They could just come change it and not have to tow you." Erik walked around Jackie and slapped his room key card on the desk.

"I would think so," Mitch added. "Make sure you ask them if they will do that when you call."

Jackie took the printed list from the desk clerk and nodded meekly as she walked over to the lobby seating area to make some calls. She was puzzled by Erik's reaction to her dilemma. Last night he had acted as though she was the most important person in the world, yet today he wouldn't spare a few minutes to help her with her crisis. Chivalry was dead.

After calling the first two numbers and finding out she would have to wait a couple of hours, she called the last person on the list, Wayne's Towing. He said he would be there in twenty minutes.

"Have any luck?" Mitch walked up with Erik close behind him.

"Yes. They're coming now so I need to get back down there." Jackie shoved the paper and her phone back in her purse.

"I'll walk down there with you," Mitch said and glanced at Erik. "I don't want you waiting in a garage alone. Did they say they could change the tire right there?"

"He said he'd have to look at it. I hope so."

The three left the hotel together but at the end of the block, Erik tapped Jackie on the shoulder. "My car's down here. I'll give you a call in a few days. Okay?" Erik seemed to wink when he flashed her a big smile and waved as he walked off.

Returning the wave, Jackie saw Mitch scowl before looking away. "Where are you parked, Mitch?"

"Oh, my wife is going to come pick me up. I'll just text her to meet us at the parking garage. I knew the parking wasn't good down here and she wanted to use the car this weekend anyway."

"I hope he can change the tire in the garage. I'd really like to get on the road soon."

"I wish I could help, but my old back couldn't take it and I haven't changed a tire since I was a young man. I'd be worried about you driving for hours on the highway on something I put on. Better to be safe."

"Oh, I understand. It's just really inconvenient when these things happen to you when you are away from home. I know a half-dozen people I could call in Carlton that would have come to fix this in a minute if I were home. Just my luck, I guess."

"How did your dinner go last night? Erik said he was taking you to the new place just down from the hotel."

"Yes, it was nice. A young crowd and the music was loud, but the food was good."

"Did Erik get a chance to tell you about Mackey Enterprises?"

"A little," Jackie shrugged. "I know his dad started the company a long time ago and he mentioned how they were expanding to include some European events."

"Yes, I've heard that." Mitch pointed to the parking sign on the corner. "Is that where you're parked?"

"Yes," Jackie nodded. "Are you not involved with the European events?"

"Oh, no. I live in a small bedroom community north of the city, and I'm just involved in the events of that area. I used to be like you. I had my own business there before I joined Mackey Enterprises. It's a big company and I don't know all the things they have going on. I just worry about my own bookings. With the holidays approaching, it's always a busy time for all event planners, isn't it?"

"Yes, it is. That's why I was hoping to get home early enough today to check on some things I have been planning."

"Did Erik talk to you about joining Mackey Enterprises?"

"No, not at all. I'm not interested in that kind of expansion. I just want to grow my business in my own area. There are other small towns around me that I think might need an event planner. I just need to get established in those areas and hire some help. I'm doing about all I can do right now as a single person business, but I've never hired any regular staff before. I've just hired help for a single event at a time. Did you have staff when you had your own business?"

"Not full time. I did like you and just hired on help when I needed it."

"That's the scary step for me. I don't know if I can generate enough business to sustain another person with a salary, but I can't grow just doing what I'm doing now. I feel kind of stuck, you know?"

"I do. My advice is that you scope out these other towns for part-time helpers and jobs first and if you think you can get the event contracts there, apply for a business loan. Then you'd have the cash to front the expansion and the salary of a second person."

"That sounds like a really good plan, Mitch. Thanks."

"You're welcome. It comes from hindsight." Mitch huffed. "It's what I wish I had done when I was in your spot. I had my wife to help me and she did pitch in anytime I needed her, but at some point, we all reach a place where we can't do any more without investing in that growth. It sounds like you have a really good area that's untapped by competition, Jackie. I encourage you to conquer it!"

"Thank you, Mitch! You should teach a motivational class at these conferences. I think you've given me the best advice yet, and I learned it in a parking garage, not a fancy hotel."

Mitch laughed shyly as Jackie waved at a tow truck coasting through the parking garage. "It looks like the tire guy is here. Thank you for staying with me. I'd be happy to give you a ride home--"

"Oh, no. The wife is on the way already. Let's just hope this guy can get you all fixed up without too much hassle."

CHAPTER SIX

Jackie was anxious to be back in Carlton. After driving for hours, the landscape had finally become familiar and she knew she was getting close. She told Stella, her opinionated navigation system, to call Calinda.

"Hey, there. Are you home?"

"Not yet, but I'm getting close. Do you have any plans for later this afternoon?"

"Like what kind of plans?" Calinda had learned long ago to be suspicious of open-ended questions from Jackie. She never answered too eagerly, or she could end up obligated for some heavy labor. Jackie was good at getting other people to do her dirty work.

"Like something your husband needs you to do. Are you going to be home doing boring stuff, or do you want to take a drive with me?"

"A drive where?" Again, Calinda was cautious. "I can't be gone long. I have to make dinner."

"Uh, I'm not putting you on a plane! I just have an errand to run, maybe an hour or so. I wanted some company. I have lots to tell you."

"Oh! In that case,... Wait, I don't have to do anything but ride along, right?"

"Right! Just go with me to the Stanley Farm and then we'll go get a drink and talk."

"The Stanley Farm? Why would you want me to go there with you? Oh, you know about Greg."

"What?" Jackie yelled at the dashboard. "No. What about Greg?"

"He's home. I haven't seen him, but I heard he was home. I don't know how long he'll stay, but I also heard he just got a divorce."

"Oh, no."

"Yeah, I guess it didn't work out and he's come home to hide out for a while. If you didn't know about that, why do you want me to tag along?"

"Good grief! Can you hear that?"

"No."

"I finally get inside the county line and there's a cop trying to pull me over!"

"Jackie, pull over!"

"I wasn't speeding. I know I wasn't. I'm using the cruise control."

"It doesn't matter! You have to pull over. I can hear it now. It's really close."

"Oh, I think it's just Larry. Why is he doing this?"

"I'm sure he has a reason." Calinda ran her hands through her hair. Jackie could be so exasperating. "Pull over and find out."

"No. He's just trying to aggravate me. He's being a bully and I'm not going to fall for that. I'm just going to ignore him."

"That's crazy, Jackie. Larry doesn't do things like that, especially not at work. If he's trying to pull you over, there's a good reason. Now just pull over and find out what it is."

"Oh, he's calling me. Can you believe that? He's calling me on the phone. Hang on. Let me see what he's got to say." Jackie stabbed the Bluetooth console to accept the incoming call. "What do you want, Larry?"

"Pull over, Jackie. I mean it. Pull over right now. NOW!"

"Good grief. What in the world..." Jackie had never heard Larry speak that way to anyone. She was too rattled to question him, so she slowed down to roll to a stop on the shoulder of the highway. Lowering her window, she looked in her side mirror to wait for him to approach. Watching closely, she saw him turn sideways in his seat and pull out crutches to lean on to help him stand. Slamming his door shut, he positioned the crutches and held up his left leg as he ambled toward her car.

Larry glared down at Jackie through the open car window. "Where have you been?"

"That's none of your business!"

Larry rolled his eyes and huffed. "Did you have some car trouble wherever you were?"

"Why, yes," Jackie said, softly. "I had a flat tire, but it's all fixed now. It was nothing."

"Whoever fixed it, didn't know what they were doing. Your tire was about to fly off of your car while you were going seventy miles an hour. You could have been killed!"

"What? No, it's just my spare, so it looks funny. My other tire is in the trunk."

"Pop your trunk." Larry didn't wait for her to argue and began hobbling to the back of her car to wait for the trunk lid to open. "Just as I thought. You don't have your tire. They took it. And you don't have your hubcap either. I'm sure they stole it, too. Right along with your license plate. Did you know you've been driving down the highway without a tag? It's a wonder you weren't pulled over long before I saw you."

"Well, don't yell at me. I didn't know." Jackie climbed from her car and walked to the back. She hadn't even noticed the license plate was missing. It could have been gone before she even went to Pittsburgh.

"You need to file a theft report. I assume you know who did this, right?"

"Yes, I called a tire service and I have their number."

"I know you probably only paid fifty bucks or so, but it's possible your tire could have been patched and now you have to buy a new one. These people shouldn't be allowed to take advantage of whoever calls them for help. You need to file the report and maybe make a complaint to the Better Business Bureau."

"Fifty dollars! I paid a lot more than that."

"I don't even want to know." Larry shook his head and slumped his shoulders. "You know, when you get in these binds, if you'd just call somebody and ask them for help--"

"It didn't happen in Carlton. I would have called someone if it had. I was out of town."

"You can still ask for help, for advice, so you don't get ripped off."

Jackie hadn't thought of calling her brother, Randy, at the time. She had expected Mitch or Erik to give her that support. "No big deal. I'll just call Randy and he'll come fix it."

"That's silly." Larry turned to go back to his squad car. "I've got a wrench. I'll tighten them, but you've got to do something about the missing plate tomorrow."

"How are you going to do this?" Jackie yelled as Larry slammed his trunk lid down. "You can't even walk. I can't believe you're working like this. What happened to your foot?"

"That's none of your business."

"Well, they shouldn't make you work like this."

Larry ignored Jackie and gingerly lowered himself to the ground in front of the wobbly tire. "You know, you could have gotten yourself killed."

"Yes, I believe you mentioned that." Jackie regretted her snide tone immediately. "I'm sorry. I don't mean to be difficult. Really, I appreciate what you're doing and that you stopped me to let me know about it."

"I'm just trying to do my job."

"I've not had a wonderful day so far and I was anxious to get home. I should have pulled over when you started following me."

"You're darn right you should have. Anybody else would have arrested you for fleeing a police officer. That's the second stupid thing you did today after hiring some thief to change your tire."

Jackie's fists were bunched at her waist. "I don't appreciate your tone, Officer Stanley."

"That's Lieutenant Stanley to you and--"

"Larry, let's not fight. I said I was sorry and--"

"I know. You're right," Larry said pulling himself up on one crutch while leaning against her car. "I'm not angry. I was afraid you were going to speed up and that tire was going to fly off. I thought I was about to see you crash."

Jackie leaned down and picked up the abandoned crutch from the ground to hand to Larry. She didn't know what to say.

"You should be okay to get home. First thing tomorrow you take your car into Schmidt's garage and get a new tire on it. That donut isn't meant for long term use."

"Well, I was going to run out to your mom's house later. I told her I'd stop in and go over the menu with her."

"I'll tell her you've had some car trouble."

"Thank you. I'll call her tomorrow and set up a new time."

Larry nodded and began to walk back to his car.

Jackie got back inside her car and knew she had lost Calinda's call, but there was a text message from her telling her to call her back. Looking in her rear-view mirror, she saw Larry waiting for her to pull back on the road. She knew he would follow her into town and somehow that made her feel better.

§

"Erik! I'm glad you called." Mitch motioned to his wife to come into the kitchen. He had been trying to think of a reason to call Erik all morning that wouldn't seem suspicious.

"Everything going all right?"

"Yeah, sure. We've got a good band for Friday and the staff are down there decorating the banquet room now. I don't foresee any problems." Mitch looked over his shoulder when he heard his wife walk in the kitchen. "I wanted to ask you about Jackie Knight."

"Oh, yeah! Did she get her tire fixed and get on her way okay?"

"Yes, a tire service showed up and they took care of everything. I wanted to ask you what your plans were. Are you inviting Jackie to join Mackey Enterprises? Or were you just interested in her on a personal level? I mean, I guess it's none of my business, but I just wanted to know in case she contacts me. I encouraged her to reach out if she had any questions or needed any advice. I don't want to speak out of turn or anything, but I just didn't know where you stood."

"I don't know yet. I'm going down there next weekend and check out her operation. I haven't made any offers. I'm not sure she has enough business to bother with, but she does sound like she's looking for answers, looking for help. I can't help her if she doesn't have enough business to help us out though. It's a two-way street."

"Yeah, I understand."

"I'll give you a heads-up if something develops. Call if you need me."

"I will. Thanks, Erik."

Mitch hung up the phone and turned to face his wife, who had listened to one side of the conversation. "He says he hasn't made any offers to her yet."

"Mitch, I still think you should warn her. She seemed like such a nice girl, and think how wonderful it would have been if someone had told us before we sold out. She might take his offer as soon as he makes it, and you won't have a chance."

"He said he's going to Ohio to check things out. I don't think he can make a move without his father's blessing, so there should still be time."

"As soon as he's gone from there, you need to call her."

"I will," Mitch said as he pulled out the kitchen chair. "I just have to think about how I can do this without getting myself in trouble. I don't need to lose my job, such that it is."

"I know, dear."

CHAPTER SEVEN

Calinda glanced over toward the window seat in her workshop when she saw Scuba sit up alert. Scuba had claimed that window seat the first time he had visited her, and now it wasn't fit for anyone else to use. As Otterhounds are known to do, Scuba liked to swim in the pond behind the house and had many times used the window seat to dry himself off. With her machines running, she couldn't hear his bark, but his whole body shook when he announced a visitor, and the movement usually caught her eye.

"Do we have company, Scuba? Or are you just wanting a snack?" Calinda's saws whined as they slowed, and she flipped up her protective mask just as Jackie walked in.

"Good morning everyone." Jackie held her arms out to her sides and glanced at Scuba. "Did the dog announce me?"

"He did," Calinda said with a chuckle. "It's getting late. I was beginning to wonder if you'd slept in today or were too busy for us."

Jackie lifted her shoulders in a heavy sigh. "I've been at Schmidt's Garage all morning. I have a new tire, but they don't have a hubcap for me. Tim said he would keep his eyes open for one and let me know if he could find a replacement."

"That's good news! Now at least you won't get in trouble with the law again." Jackie had called her after she'd gotten home and told her about the encounter with Larry on the highway.

"Except I still don't have a license plate! I guess I'll do that this afternoon and then I'm putting this whole miserable event behind me." Jackie waved her hands to demonstrate brushing the troubles aside as her metal bracelets clanged together. "It was a messy end to a rather interesting week. Finding my perfect man was worth the cost of the conference alone."

"The perfect man, huh?"

"Wait until you see him, Calinda. Since we were teenagers, I've described this man to you and you'll see it with one look. He is everything I've always talked about. He's perfect for me!"

"Perfect, huh? Hmm," Calinda walked behind the bar in the back of the workshop. "Do you want some coffee?"

Jackie nodded and moved to take a barstool, plopping her purse down on the stool beside her. "He's educated and dressed like he stepped out of a GQ magazine. He's confident and charming. He's successful and--"

"But does he worship the ground you walk on?" Calinda smiled and raised her eyebrow. "As I recall, that was a requirement that was pretty high on your list." Even as teenagers, Jackie had outlined the perfect man to Calinda. She used to point them out in fashion magazines when she saw a picture of a viable candidate. She was attracted to a man in a well-fitted suit, tall and slim, but even as she pointed them out, she would always add that they would worship the ground she walked on.

"At this point, he is highly interested. We've only spent a few days together. That full capture doesn't happen overnight."

"Isn't it going to be hard to cultivate that at a distance?"

"He's coming here next weekend. He probably can't stay long, but I'll have his undivided attention since he doesn't know anyone else. The problem we kept having at the conference is that he was running the thing, so we kept getting interrupted."

"Must I remind you that you are running the Chamber Christmas dance?"

"Ah," Jackie waved her hand. "I can run that with my eyes shut."

"I think that's the best way to get through it." Calinda teased. She had never been fond of these public events and seeing all of the Carlton residents dressed in their fanciest attire could range from comical to sad sometimes.

"All teasing aside, Calinda, this guy is really special. I could never find a guy like him around here. He's polished and he's going somewhere. He's motivated to grow and improve. He wants to expand his company and he's willing to work to create something. The guys around here just get a job out of high school and plug along until they die. It's so depressing."

"But if he's going somewhere, are you going there, too? It doesn't sound like this is a guy who would ever consider living in Carlton, Ohio. He's not going to be a small-town person. He's always going to need a city, and his job is going to come first. Is that really something that would make you happy?"

"I didn't think so. I never thought I'd leave here. I do want to expand and have events in the towns around here, but I haven't ever thought of leaving. At least, not until now. Now I see that I could work with Erik and we would do events together. It would be something we would share. I've never dated anyone who was interested in my work before or my events. They usually see it as an inconvenience because I have to attend events at night or weekends when other people are off work. That's just another reason why Erik is so perfect."

"I don't know, Jackie. It's really hard for people to be together twenty-four hours a day. A lot of people find it difficult to even work with their spouse. You could get sick of each other pretty quick, and then you're off in some city you don't want to live in without anyone."

"I'm not packing my bags yet," Jackie said with a smirk. "There's a lot of untapped territory here in eastern Ohio. Erik said so himself! He knows I have no competition at all around here and he seems very intrigued by that. I'm hoping he will consider moving here to Carlton and using it as a base location to develop eastern Ohio for his father. Then--"

"Then you get your way." Calinda laughed.

"Exactly."

"Silly me. I should have known you had a plan."

"Of course I do." Jackie took a sip of her coffee.

"So, you didn't tell me about your last night. You went to the French restaurant, the bar down the street and where did he take you the last night you were in Pittsburgh?"

"A wedding reception." Jackie paused for Calinda's reaction and grinned when her eyes grew wide. "I know. I know it sounds crazy, but it was the best date of all! His company was managing the whole wedding and reception so we stopped in. He first wanted to just make sure everything was going okay, but they had a big disco dance floor, a great band, plenty of food and an open bar, so we stayed. It was a blast! The wedding party was huge so nobody even noticed us and Erik is a great dancer. It was so much fun to be at an event like that and know that I didn't have to check with the caterer or pay attention to how long the band took a break. It wasn't my thing, so I got to just enjoy it."

"That's great, Jackie. I'm glad you had a good time."

"So, what did I miss around here? Anything happen?"

"Actually, yes." Calinda cocked her head sideways.

"Really? What?"

"Well, it's not happy news, but the Parkers lost their home. There was a fire and they are okay, but they can't live in the house without some serious renovations. With winter here there's no way they'll be able to work on it now. Your brother, Randy, told me that a group of men were going over there to try to cover it with tarps to keep water from doing any more damage. It's supposed to snow tomorrow."

"So, where did Tom and Betty go? Where are they staying?"

"Nolan is letting them stay in his house on Maple Trail. It's for sale, but it's just sitting empty."

"They have a son still at home, don't they?"

"Yeah, they have a son in high school. He wasn't home when the fire started. I thought it was a brush fire, but Randy said they think it started in the chimney. Nolan's been working on getting them set up over there. They need everything and he's got a lot of extra stuff in storage that he's getting out for them. That's what all that is over there." Calinda pointed to the corner of the workshop where cardboard boxes were stacked next to an open plastic tote filled with dishes and kitchen tools.

"I can't believe that. How awful for them, especially at the holidays."

"I know. Betty was pretty upset."

"If Nolan wants to load all of that in my car, I'll drive it over to them when I leave here. I want to go by and check on them anyway."

"I think one of the guys is coming by for it, but I'll ask him."

"Maybe we could have a fundraiser for them? Or a house raising when springtime comes?"

"I don't know if Tom would go for that." Calinda looked up the stairway to the house when she heard the door open.

"I could check and see if there's something I could incorporate into the Christmas dance. Maybe take up a collection for them at the vendor fair or later that night at the party. I'm sure there's something we can do."

"Are you talking about the Parkers?" Nolan said as he walked down the stairs.

Calinda nodded.

"I hadn't thought about that, but you're right, Jackie," Nolan said. "Maybe there's something we can do to help the Parkers. I'm not really sure what they need. I keep trying to ask and Tom just says they are fine. They can't be fine. They don't even have any clothes!"

"I was just going up to tell you that Jackie can take your boxes over there. She's going to check on the Parkers when she leaves here."

"Yeah. If you'll load them in my car for me, I'll take them." Jackie said.

Nolan nodded and stacked two boxes together. "Can you grab the door for me, honey? It's easier than going up the steps back here."

Calinda rushed over to the door to hold it open. Scuba stood up briefly, but then decided Nolan didn't really need his help, so he returned to his morning nap.

"Are you going to the Stanley Farm today?" Calinda said once Nolan was out the door.

"Yes, I told Barbara that I would stop by, but I didn't give her a time. I'll drive out there after I visit Betty."

"You might run into Larry again," Calinda said with a wince.

"I won't stop if his car is there. I don't want to hear him preaching at me again about highway safety. He's probably already told his mother the story of how I wouldn't pull over when he tried to stop me yesterday."

"You know you should have. He's right."

"Of course, he's right! Larry is always right. He's the authority on everything. You have to do everything his way. He's..." Jackie fluttered her hands in the air exasperated that she couldn't find the words.

"He's just like you." Calinda nodded.

"What?! I'm not like that. I don't know everything." Jackie sneered.

"But you do want everyone to do as you say." Calinda raised an eyebrow. "Don't give me that look. You know what I'm talking about."

"Well, maybe." Jackie cracked a smile. "But I only have your best interest at heart." Batting her eyelashes to feign sincerity, she gave into laughter when Calinda rolled her eyes.

"Yeah, right. Isn't it going to be awkward doing Christmas for them when you and Larry don't get along?"

"I was toying with the idea of hiring someone part-time to go in my place. I'll do all the work to set it up, but they could go to the event and just call me if they had any problems. I haven't found the right person for the job yet though."

"You may have a hard time finding someone to work on Christmas Eve. What are you planning to do for Christmas Day? You can come over here and eat with us. I'm going to cook a turkey."

"I don't want to be a third wheel and I may have to go to the Stanley's. It doesn't matter. It's just another workday for me. Larry will just have to stay away from me."

"Oh, I'm sure that will work," Calinda said sarcastically.

"Well, if everyone will just do what I say..." Jackie leaned an elbow on the bar.

Both girls were laughing when Nolan opened the door to make another trip to Jackie's car. "Don't tell me," Nolan said, holding out his hands in front of him. "I don't want to know."

CHAPTER EIGHT

Jackie stepped gingerly through the gravel trying not to turn her ankle in heels just as her cell phone chirped to announce the arrival of a text. When she safely reached the porch of the Stanley Farm, she pulled her phone from her purse and saw a text from Erik.

Thinking of you. Will call tonight.

Jackie smiled at the tingling flutter his message caused in her heart and slipped the phone back into her bag. A new love was so exciting, and Erik had turned out to be such a romantic. Finding flowers in her hotel room and notes tucked under her door in the morning had convinced her that his interest was sincere. He had been so attentive that she thought sure he was a strong candidate for her perfect match.

She had always joked with Calinda about wanting to be worshiped, but all she really wanted was someone who was thoughtful and caring. She wasn't a teenager anymore and the men she had dated so far were always unable to accept her work hours and they kept her at arm's length. Her only living family member was her younger brother, Randy, and she wanted to belong somewhere. She wanted her own family and to have someone she could count on to think about her once in a while.

The incident with the tire on the highway had started her thinking about how long it might take before someone registered her absence. If that tire had come off of her car when she'd been driving and caused her to wreck her car before she reached home, she could have been hospitalized in a dozen different towns between Carlton, Ohio and Pittsburgh. How long would it have been before someone noticed that she hadn't come home on time? Calinda was the only person she'd told.

"Jackie! I thought I heard a car outside. Come on inside, dear. The wind is getting chilly. They say we might get snow tonight."

"Good morning, Mrs. Stanley. How are you today?" Jackie followed the woman inside and shut the front door.

"Call me Barbara. I'm a little stiff today, but I expect that's due to the weather. What did you bring me?" Barbara Stanley fell back into her vinyl-clad recliner and motioned for Jackie to sit.

"I have the menu we talked about, and I want your final approval before I give it to the caterers." Jackie pulled her notebook from her purse and handed the list to Mrs. Stanley. "I had another idea for entertainment that I wanted to run by you."

"Is that mashed potatoes? Where's my glasses?" Barbara slapped the table beside her chair and rocked forward to look around the room. "There," she said, pointing. "Can you grab those for me, honey?"

Jackie saw the glasses on the kitchen counter and jumped up to get them for her.

"Thank you."

"You're welcome. I think I told you that I wasn't able to get the piano that we rented last year."

"Yeah. I think we can just play music though. That'll be okay." Mrs. Stanley tapped the list in front of her. "Are those yams on here? I really liked those last year."

"Yes, ma'am. They're on there. I heard they were a favorite."

"Did Larry tell you?" Barbara Stanley looked up over her reading glasses and grinned. "He was real fond of them, too."

"Yes, he said he was."

"Have you talked to him lately?" Barbara dropped the list in her lap and looked at Jackie.

"Yeah, actually I saw him last night."

"Oh, you did, did you?" Barbara Stanley asked with a high-pitched lilt to her voice. "Where did you run into him at?"

"I'm surprised he didn't tell you. I had a problem with a tire on my car and he helped me out."

"Oh, you're right. He did tell me you weren't able to come yesterday because you had a problem with your car. I thought he was just giving me a message. I didn't know he was helping you with it."

"Yes, he helped me."

"He's good with cars," Barbara said. "He doesn't have the patience to do it for a living, but he can fix basic stuff. Now Greg, my youngest, he's the one that likes to work with all the little pieces. He can fuss with the smallest detail and always liked taking everything apart when he was a kid, but not Larry. Larry's a helper and a problem solver. I guess they both found their right place in life."

"Yes, well, about the entertainment," Jackie said, squirming in her seat. She didn't want to talk about Larry. "Do you know what a karaoke machine is? It's a--"

"Yeah, I've heard of them. I've not seen one, but I know they're a microphone for people to sing into. I think Sonny Miles had one at his daughter's wedding reception. The boys talked about it."

"Yes, it plays a popular song and gives you the lyrics so you can sing along. I thought it might be fun for your event if I could rent one. Then your family could play around with it. If everyone's too shy to sing, it will always play music for you."

"Hey, that sounds fun. Let's give it a try. Does it do Christmas songs?"

"I'll see what I can do. I think I can rent one over in Barnesville. I thought it might be fun for everyone." Jackie reached out and took the menu back from Mrs. Stanley and put it in her purse. "If you think of anything else you need, get in touch with me right away. We've only got a few days left to make changes." Jackie stood up. "The furniture movers are coming early on Thursday to take your furniture out and bring in the tables and chairs. I thought that might be easier than doing it the night before like we did last year."

"Oh, good. I'll be up early."

"Okay," Jackie said as she tied the belt of her coat. "I'll get on it."

"Jackie," Barbara Stanley reached out her hand and Jackie stopped. "Can I tell you something?"

"Sure." Jackie lowered herself back to the chair.

"I have always been able to tell when something is right. Do you know what I mean?"

Jackie frowned.

"I can just feel it in my bones. It's a gift from God or maybe a curse." Barbara chuckled. "I can't tell sometimes, but I've just always been able to do it. There are a lot of changes that happen in life. Some you control and some you don't, but I can just tell when it's a good change or a bad one. My husband, Lawrence, didn't trust my instincts at first, but over the years he learned to know they were real. He'd even ask me, 'Barbie, what do you think?' and I'd tell him."

"Well, that must be a handy superpower to have." Jackie smiled, not certain where the story was going.

"My youngest boy, Greg, he's made some decisions in his life and seen some changes. Some good, some bad. I try to help with those decisions, but he hasn't learned to trust my instincts. He thinks I'm an old woman who doesn't understand what he's going through. I could have saved him a lot a heartache."

Jackie nodded. "Sometimes we only learn from making our own mistakes."

"Perhaps so, but it's hard as a mother to watch it happen."

"I'm sure it is." Jackie reached over to pat Barbara's hand.

"So, when I have to sit here and watch it happen, I feel like I need to at least try to say something, even if nobody listens to me."

"I can certainly understand that." Jackie put her purse on her shoulder feeling the story was nearing the end.

"That's why I have to say that you made a big mistake breaking up with my boy, Larry. It may not be my place to say so. I'm not your momma, but I just feel better if I get it said."

"I don't have anything against your son, Mrs. Stanley. We just weren't right for each other."

"Poppycock!" Mrs. Stanley's feet flew out in front of her and swung back against the recliner. "That's where you're wrong. You need to fix this before it's too late."

"I'm afraid it's already too late." Jackie smiled and stood up. "I'm seeing someone else now and I'm sure Larry is better off, but

I appreciate your support. You know I love your whole family, and there's nothing I would have liked more than to be a part of the Stanleys, but we just weren't a good fit."

Barbara shook head. "We would have loved having you, too."

"Thank you."

§

"Hey, mom. You here?" Larry Stanley yelled as the screen door slammed behind him.

Barbara yelled back from the living room. "In here."

"I'm making a sandwich. You want anything?"

Barbara walked in the kitchen to find Larry removing things from the refrigerator and sliding them on the counter as he hopped on one foot. "You just missed Jackie. She stopped by with my holiday menu."

"Yeah, I saw her." Larry pushed the door shut and grabbed a loaf of bread. "You want a sandwich?"

"No, thank you." Barbara pulled a stool out from the bar and stepped up on the rung to sit down. "Did you talk to Jackie?"

"No. I just passed her car."

"She told me that you helped her last night. She had car trouble?"

Larry snorted. "Yeah, I helped her."

Barbara leaned forward trying to make eye contact with her stubborn son. "Why do you say it like that? What happened?"

"Nothing. I pulled her over because her wheel was wobbling. The lug nuts were loose."

"That's dangerous. I'm sure she appreciated that."

Larry opened a drawer to get a knife and pressed the sandwich down before cutting it. "Just doing my job."

"Jackie told me that she's seeing someone." Barbara watched closely for a reaction, but Larry did not give her one. "Did you know that?"

"Hmm? No, but that's good."

"Pfft, you don't mean that. I told her she was making a mistake. The two of you don't know right from wrong."

"Mom, please don't get involved. I know you think a lot of Jackie, but that just didn't work out and you need to forget about it."

"It's not something you just forget about, Larry. It's --"

"What are you guys arguing about?" Greg Stanley walked into the kitchen in pajama pants and scratched his stubbly chin.

"Are you just getting up? Good grief." Larry huffed.

"I wouldn't be up yet if you weren't in here bickering. What's he done now, Mom?"

"We were just talking about Jackie Knight. She stopped by earlier."

Larry hopped to the table with his sandwich and Barbara slid down from her barstool and followed with his drink.

"Jackie was here! Why didn't you wake me up? I haven't seen Jackie since I've been back, and I looked for her when I went down to the high school. I thought maybe she would be down there getting things ready for the dance."

"Why are you looking for Jackie?" Larry said as he turned around in his seat.

"I heard she was available. I've had a crush on Jackie Knight since I was fifteen. Where have you been?"

"Boys, none of that matters." Barbara handed Larry a napkin. "And Greg, you don't even have your life worked out yet. You don't need to be chasing Jackie or anyone else."

"Yeah, that's right." Larry nodded at his mother. "She's not available. She's seeing somebody anyway."

"What? Who?" Greg opened the cabinet for a cup and reached for the coffee pot.

Larry looked at his mother and shrugged.

"I didn't ask her. She just said she was seeing someone now." Barbara placed her hand on Larry's arm. "I still think you should ask her to the Christmas dance."

"Mom! I'm not going to do that." Larry shook his head and patted his mother's hand.

"I could," Greg said, stirring sugar into his coffee. "I could ask her. I'll give her a call."

"Please don't do that," Barbara said turning in her chair. "You don't need to do anything right now other than take care of your own marriage."

"She filed for divorce!"

"But you aren't divorced yet," Barbara stood up and pushed her chair under the table. "Take care of that relationship first."

"There's nothing left to do there." Greg joined Larry at the table and shrugged when Barbara left the kitchen. "That ship has sailed."

"I'm sorry about that," Larry said.

"Nah, it's okay. So, what's with mom and Jackie?"

"Nothing. Mom just likes her, and she can't let it go."

"But you can?"

"I already have." Larry's sandwich was gone, and he crumpled his napkin in his hands as he pushed back his chair. "As you would say, that ship has sailed."

"So, you don't care if I call her?"

Larry stood on his right leg and reached for his crutches. "I can't recommend the journey, but you can make your own choices."

"I can sure make 'em." Greg chuckled. "So far I haven't done such a great job at that though."

Larry nodded. Maybe he hadn't done any better than his little brother. He had once thought Jackie was his future, but he had never been good enough for her. She would not be content as a local cop's wife. She had big dreams and he didn't fit anywhere.

"See ya later, Mom." Larry didn't wait for an answer before heading out the front door.

CHAPTER NINE

With her new license plate in her back seat, Jackie headed toward the local radio station, WBNC. She had promised her friend, Missy, some tickets to sell for the Christmas dance, and after talking with Betty Parker, she knew Missy would help her ask the community for help.

When she entered the tiny radio station lobby, she saw Hank in the soundproof booth, and he waved to her. No one was in the lobby, so she walked down the only hallway until she found Missy in a back office.

"Hey, Jackie. Come on in. I've got fifteen minutes before I'm up. What have you got for me?"

Missy was Hank's wife and they ran the station together with live talk in the mornings and pre-recorded programming the rest of the day. Hank handled weather and general news reports, but Missy dug into the local happenings, interviewing elected officials, and promoting events. She could be cold-blooded when she needed to be, but over the years she had been softened by Jackie's whimsy and eagerly shared any events she was planning.

"Well, I brought you some dance tickets, so you can offer them on the air, but I have another mission I'm hoping you can throw some support toward."

"It's Christmastime, girl. My chat is pretty full. What's your current quest?"

"I'm sure you heard about the Parker's house."

"Yeah, Hank got the report on that. Horrible shame. They're good people and it couldn't have happened at a worse time."

"I agree. Calinda Willow, well Calinda Ramsey now, has put them up in her husband's empty house. You know the old Crawford place on Maple Trail?"

Missy nodded.

"They can stay there, and it's partially furnished. The problem is that they need clothing and personal items. Their bedroom was a complete loss. They left with the clothes on their back."

"Wow, devastating. So, you want to collect stuff for them?"

"I do. I brought a list of sizes and drop off places. If you have a box to put in the lobby and are willing, you can add the station to the drop off list. The list may grow, but right now I've only talked to the post office, drugstore, and The Villa. They are all putting out a collection box. There will be one at the vendor show and the dance as well. I want to make it convenient to everyone because people get in a rush around the holidays and don't have much time to run extra places. The drugstore put a jar on the counter for money donations too, because Betty has medication needs."

"All good ideas. Yeah, we can put a box in the lobby here and I'll call you if it fills up."

"Tom is being pretty stubborn about all this and doesn't want to accept help, but Betty is a realist and she is thankful. They always help everyone else, so I hope to see the folks here step up."

"Gotcha." Missy ran around her desk and out the office door with Jackie following.

"Text me if you need anything."

"Will do and email me the town's New Years Eve plans. I know you have that info, and the mayor's office never remembers to send them to me. I want to start announcing that on the 26th."

Although Missy ran inside the booth before Jackie could answer, she gave her a thumbs up as she pushed through the station door.

§

The next morning, Jackie pushed through the workshop door in the back of Calinda's house, stomped her feet on the door mat, and held her arms out to her sides to receive the anticipated announcement of her arrival. As expected, Scuba sat up on his front paws and threw his head back in a mournful baying sound that always sent Calinda into a fit of giggles. Taking a bow, Jackie walked over to the bar. "That dog does make a weird sound. Is it just me? Or does everyone get that long deep moaning noise when they walk in?"

"Most everyone," Calinda said with a shrug. "That's just an Otterhound sound. He can't help it."

"I don't know how you take it." Jackie shook her head. "Now, I have a million things to do. I need to make some notes. It just dawned on me, why are you down here working? It's almost Christmas. You don't usually work in December."

"I'm not working, really. I'm just playing. My orders have all been shipped but I'm playing around with some new ideas. It doesn't feel like work to me." Calinda placed a coffee mug on the counter. "Nolan's working upstairs and I don't want to disturb him. Is everything going okay with the dance?"

"Yes. I'm happy to say it's running smoothly. We had some minor decorating problems, but that's all been straightened out now. Do you have more stuff that needs to go to Betty's?" Jackie pointed at the boxes by the back door.

"Nolan found some sheets, blankets and pillows that need to go over there."

"I can take them. I've got to run back over there anyway, and I should still have enough room to add them. I picked up some things from the drugstore. Chester called me this morning and said that Leona Pryor sent her nephew down there with six boxes of clothes for Tom. He didn't have anywhere to put the boxes and he needed me to come get them. She heard about the collection on the radio, and she still has all of her husband's stuff in storage. He was about Tom's size, so they should be a big help. She even had shoes and a coat for him. I hope it all fits."

"That's great. Anything for Betty?"

"Not yet, but I haven't picked up from any of the other locations. I'm going to take what I have now and then check back with everyone at the end of the day to see if I need to pick up from them. After I drop this off, I've got to run over to Barnesville and pick up a karaoke machine. I rented it for the Stanley party, but they don't deliver. Do you know how to hook those things up? I've never done it."

"Well, I sure can't help you. You'll probably have to look it up on the internet. It's more than just a machine though. Doesn't it have speakers and microphones and all that? How do they make the lyrics show upon the wall? I've seen one, but I have no idea how it works."

Jackie rested her forehead in her palm. "I'll have to worry about that later. I can't get a minute to think. There's so much going on at once. I've got to get my own house in order and figure out what I'm going to wear. Erik will be here in a few days and I'm a mess."

"So, he's still coming?"

"Yes! Of course he's still coming. Why did you say it like that?" Jackie eyed her suspiciously.

"Well, the snow, the holiday," Calinda shrugged her shoulders. "I didn't know..."

Jackie huffed. "He calls me every night and sends me emails about his work. He's a very busy guy."

"I'm sure. That's what I meant. The holiday events must be pretty intense right now." Calinda busied herself behind the bar cleaning up the drips around the coffee pot.

"He just oversees now. He has other people that do the grunt work. I wish I could be so lucky."

Calinda smiled. "You would be bored. The only way that would work is if you could sit on a high stool and direct every step they take. Even then, no one could please you. I can't imagine you going off somewhere and just letting other people run your events."

"Hmm, when you put it that way, it does seem a little hard to imagine."

"You actually like going to all those parties," Calinda said with a shudder.

"Of course, I do! I would definitely want to be at all of them, but I would like some help setting them up."

"You'll eventually find that person. You just need to keep looking. I thought about that last night. You said something the other day about how guys around here get out of school and just take a job they can do."

"Yeah, and they stay there their whole life doing exactly the same thing."

"And it dawned on me then. That's where you need to catch them!"

"What?" Jackie shook her head until her long dangling earrings slapped her cheek.

"The high school!" Calinda pounded her fist on the counter. "You need to recruit."

"You're not making any sense. Are we talking about finding men or employees?"

"Employees!" Calinda gasped.

"Oh, I see your point." Jackie relaxed a bit and then frowned. "You think I need to hire students? I have a few times for decorating jobs or help with errands."

"I mean you need to participate in the career fair the high school has every spring. You just put up a table and the upper classmen can stop and ask questions about what you do or what you're looking for. You'd meet a lot of kids that aren't college bound but are looking for something special. You may meet the perfect party personality right there. I bet the high schools in the neighboring towns have the same fairs and you could go there, too."

Jackie hummed and raised her eyebrows. "Not a bad idea. I can't believe I didn't think of that."

Calinda laughed. "You probably should ask the principal. I bet he knows what students like to organize functions at the school. If someone had asked when we were in school, the principal would have pointed right at you. People that have that quality, tend to show it early."

"Yes, I was a star, even as a child." Jackie tossed her head back. "The principal knew my name for more than one reason."

Calinda raised an eyebrow. "Yes, and he never knew me at all."

"Goody two-shoes." Jackie sneered at Calinda before they both laughed. "Ah, the good old days!"

CHAPTER TEN

"This is just ugly." Mitch's wife, Sandy, dropped her head and muttered something Mitch didn't hear.

"What's wrong?" Putting his arm around her shoulders, Mitch patted her arm.

"This box that Pamela dropped off. This is what she wants us to use for Lindsey's party. I can't believe how tacky it looks. I'm embarrassed to even put it up."

"We can't keep putting money into a business we don't own. You know we decided we weren't buying anything else. It's the responsibility of Mackey Enterprises to provide these things or compensate us for it if they can't. When she drops something off, we have to use it."

"I know. I know, Mitch, but this stuff is so inappropriate for the occasion. I'd rather go without decorations than use this. Maybe we have something in our garage that we could use. I won't buy anything, but we are not going to have any bookings if we don't do something about this problem." Sandy picked up a plastic wall decoration of a pink treble clef with a crushed red bow around it. "What in the world would you use this for? A music recital on Valentine's Day? I mean, really, Mitch. It's almost like they want us to fail."

"Perhaps they do." Mitch gave her a knowing look. "I've been thinking about it since this last conference. Erik said some things that made me curious and Pamela was just cold to me the whole time."

"She is always on the edge of being rude anyway. I can see why she's never been actively involved in the customer side of the business."

"I think that's why she's so cranky. Her father has situated her in a career that doesn't suit her. Maybe someday she will find her place."

"What did Erik say last weekend that made you think he wants you to fail?" Sandy tossed the ugly pink wall hanging to the side and reached down in the box.

"Maybe it's nothing," Mitch tilted his head to the right. "Maybe I'm sensitive, but a couple of times he started a sentence by saying, 'When you retire...' or 'Once you retire...'. That type of thing tells me he is certainly expecting me to do that soon."

"Did you tell him you don't plan to do that anytime soon?"

"No. I didn't say anything. I don't want to rock the boat. I don't know why he would want that though. We do a good job up here in Glenshaw. He doesn't have anybody else up here in this area to handle Glenshaw events."

"That's true." Sandy nodded and held up a small cluster of plastic roses before dropping them in the discard pile next to her.

"Somehow, I felt like he wanted it to happen. He wants me to retire. Maybe he's got his eye on someone he wants to replace me."

"Do you think it's Jackie?"

"No. She doesn't want to leave Ohio. She made that clear to him. I don't know who else he might be wining and dining right now."

"He should just bring them in, and they can work with us. Then they'll have it all once you do retire." Sandy continued sorting through the decorations box and making two piles.

"That wouldn't really work with his pitch. He presents it like you are getting promoted. You are getting a territory of your own to be a vice president of the company. You feel like it's a step up, so it wouldn't really work if you were assigned to work with someone else or there was somebody already working in your territory."

"Oh, I see."

"I wonder if he's wanting to hire that young girl. There was a young girl at the conference who came alone. She seemed really shy. I tried to talk to her a few times, but she seemed nervous. I know she lived north of the city, but I don't know where exactly. Maybe he wants to offer her the Glenshaw area."

"Sounds like she could benefit from working with someone else." Sandy scooped up everything in the unacceptable pile and tossed them in the large cardboard box that Pamela had dropped off.

"He couldn't play the ego card then. I've seen him work and I'm embarrassed to say it worked on me, too. He plays on people's ego with flattery and they usually fall in line. At least I'm not the only sucker."

"That's why it's important that you warn Jackie." Sandy pointed her finger at Mitch as he picked up the box of discards and carried them to the table by the door of the banquet room.

"I'm not sure she'll listen. You always think that bad stuff happens to other people and that what you have is real. She may not believe me."

"Maybe it needs to be me," Sandy said with her hands on her hips. "I was thinking about that after you spoke with Erik on the telephone. Maybe Jackie would take it better from me. It might be less humiliating and more believable."

"I hate to drag you into this."

"You're not." Sandy put her arms around Mitch's neck. "I liked Jackie, too, although I only met her briefly in the parking garage. I understand why you want to help her, and I feel the same way. I'm going to give her a call on Monday, after Erik's trip up there."

Mitch nodded and kissed Sandy's forehead. "Maybe I'll give her a call today, just to say hi. Keep communication open and then it won't seem so strange when we call her next week."

Sandy nodded. "Now, let's run home and look in the garage. I know I have blue tablecloths in there that we can use, and maybe those white floating candles we used at the Herschel wedding reception would look pretty. Lindsey doesn't want this party to have a Christmas theme, so nothing red."

"Okay. Let's go take a look." Mitch handed Sandy her coat and they locked up the banquet room for the quick trip home.

"Good morning," Erik's voice blared through the speakers of Jackie's SUV when she tapped the phone icon. "Am I calling at a bad time?"

"No, not at all. I'm just driving." Jackie felt her heartbeat in her throat at the sound of his voice. "I'm going to a nearby town to pick up a karaoke machine that I rented."

"Oh, are you using that this weekend?"

"No, it's for a party next week, but the business will be closed for the holidays, so I have to pick it up early. What are you doing today?"

"Just the normal pre-Christmas stuff. Checking my lists and checking them twice." Erik chuckled. "I was calling to see how much snow you got last night. I know you said it was snowing when we talked but I can't seem to get accurate weather information on Carlton, Ohio from here."

"I guess we're too small. The snow wasn't bad. We might have a couple of inches but it's soft stuff, no ice."

"Good, so no trouble driving?"

"Not at all. I'm on the highway now and it's all clear. Did you get snow?"

"Yeah, I woke to about the same thing. Nothing troubling. I'll see you soon."

"Okay." Jackie smiled and felt a tingling glow. "I'll see you soon." He had such a sexy voice; a long-distance relationship just might work.

After seeing a billboard advertising a Barnesville air conditioning company, Jackie knew she was very close to town when her Bluetooth screen rang again.

"Hello."

"Hey, Jackie! It's Mitch. Just checking in to see how your Christmas party planning is coming."

"Hi, Mitch! It's funny you should call. I was just thinking about you this morning. I'm on my way right now to pick up a karaoke machine for a party next week and I don't have a clue how to set this thing up. I thought maybe it was something you would know about."

"Oh, yeah. I've got one of my own. I bought it before Mackey Enterprises bought my business." Mitch covered the phone receiver with his hand, but Jackie could still hear him tell his wife about the karaoke machine. "Sorry, Sandy's here and I was just telling her what you got. We've had a blast with that thing. I'm certainly no singer, but plenty of people have used ours and they sound pretty good. It's a lot of laughs."

"I think it might be a hit for a family reunion that I have on Christmas Eve. The problem is that I don't really know exactly what I'm picking up or what to do with it when I get to the venue. Does it come with everything? I just plug it in?"

"It's pretty simple. There are many different models but most of the small units have a screen with them, like a monitor, and that's where the lyrics scroll. There should be speakers and microphones with stands. It may seem like a lot of pieces, but it goes together pretty quickly. Hopefully, they give you instructions and all the parts. After you get home with it, send me a screen shot of what they gave you and I can give you a little more specifics on it. Sandy can help you, too, if you get to the party and something isn't working right."

"Thank you, and thank Sandy, too. This is the reason I wanted to go to a conference. I wanted to make friends with people who have the same struggles I have." Jackie chuckled. "Or maybe people who knew how to help me with mine."

"Always happy to help!"

"Are you working on a Christmas party this weekend?"

"Right now, Sandy and I are decorating for a non-Christmas party tonight. The young lady is having a wedding shower and she doesn't want any Christmas themed items there, so we are looking through our stash to see what we can find for her. Tomorrow we have a children's Christmas party in the afternoon and an employee Christmas party that evening for one of our local businesses. We're helping our church Sunday evening with a reception and then we're clear for the week. It's going to be a full weekend, but then we get to have a quiet Christmas with family."

"Wow, that does sound like a crazy weekend. My karaoke debut is Christmas Eve, so I'll try to make sure I know how to get this thing running before the party, so I don't have to bother you. Then I can relax on Christmas day."

"The life of an event planner means you're never alone on a holiday!" Mitch chuckled.

"I'll check back with you after the weekend. Good luck with your party."

"Thanks, Mitch. Talk to you soon."

A wave of melancholy gripped Jackie. She may be rarely alone on a holiday, but somehow, she was always lonely.

CHAPTER ELEVEN

Jackie drove slowly down Maple Trail to avoid the pot holes because her SUV was full to the brim with donation boxes, Nolan's bedding, and the karaoke machine that wanted to dance around in the middle seat every time she hit a bump. People had teased her for buying such a large SUV when she was a single woman without kids, but no one realized how much equipment and decorations she had to haul around everywhere. She was thankful for the large interior and the seat that folded down flat, but it was definitely time to unload. She may have more to pick up before the day was over.

Vowing to rearrange the karaoke machine once the clothing boxes were removed, Jackie pulled to the side of the road in front of the house where Tom and Betty were staying and in front of Larry's white truck. Larry Stanley was leaning against the truck with his crutches under his arms and yelling at someone on the roof of the house.

"Hey," Jackie said as she gingerly stepped between the vehicles. She wanted to be cordial, but she didn't want to interact with Larry if it wasn't required. Putting her hand up over her eyes to shield the sun bouncing off the snow, she saw a figure on the roof. She pulled her sunglasses down her nose to peer over the top and thought it looked like Larry's brother. "Is that Greg up there?"

"Hey," Larry said casually over his shoulder and then cupped his hands around his mouth to yell. "It sags too much on the left. You've got to tighten it up."

Jackie walked up beside Larry and looked up.

"Yeah, that's Greg. I'm supervising." Larry pointed at the roof.

"You're putting up lights on the house?" Jackie squinted. "Wow. Christmas lights?"

"Yeah, you know mom has too much of this stuff. The whole attic and another storage building out by the barn is full of holiday decorations. She got a bunch of stuff together for me to haul over here. I can't really get up a ladder right now, so little brother had to get up there."

"That is so nice of her to think of this. I've always wanted Christmas lights on my house. I just never had time and it seems like I'm never home. I love to look at them though. Your mom always has beautiful lights at Christmas."

"It may not be as good as usual this year because he had to do them." Larry pointed up again and chuckled. "I've got tree decorations in here, too. I guess I'll run out and get them a tree once he's finished up there. That'll give Betty something to do."

"Hey, Jackie!" Greg Stanley stood on the roof and waved his hand over his head.

"Hi, Greg." Jackie waved back and saw Greg head for the ladder. "Well, I've got a bunch of boxes in my car. Leona Pryor donated some clothing for Tom and Nolan sent some bedding. I'm out of room and I need to unload because there may be more to pick up later."

"Hey, Jackie. It's great to see you." Greg reached out to embrace Jackie and she looked quizzically over his shoulder at Larry. Larry just shrugged and looked up. He knew Jackie didn't care a whit for Greg. They barely knew each other, and Jackie had no idea about Greg's teenage crush.

"It's good to see you, too."

Greg stepped back and looked at Jackie up and down from head to toe. "You look great!"

"Thank you." Jackie paused and the silence was awkward. "I've got some boxes to drop off in my car."

"Oh, here! Let me help. I can carry that in for you." Jackie pushed the button on her key fob to get the door to raise and Greg rubbed his hands together. "These boxes?"

"Yes, there are six boxes in the back, and I'll get the stuff in the middle seat."

Greg grabbed a box and headed for the front door of the house as Jackie opened the side door of her SUV. Grabbing the bags full of pillows, she walked by Larry. "Greg really has the Christmas spirit."

"Oh yes," Larry said with a wry smile. "He's quite the happy little elf."

Jackie frowned again because she didn't understand the sarcasm. Something odd was going on with those two and she didn't want to get involved.

"Hey, Jackie." Greg waited by the door as Jackie placed the pillows on the couch. "Do you have a date for the Christmas dance? Because if you don't, I'd be happy to be your escort. I'm just back in town and I don't have anyone to go with."

"Thank you, but I have a date already. I bet I could find you someone to go with if that's what you'd like. I hear the same thing from lots of people. They'd like to go, but they don't want to go alone. I could give you some suggestions."

"Really? It won't be as good as going with you, but do you have anyone hot I could ask?"

Jackie giggled as she stepped out of the front door and headed down the sidewalk with Greg at her heels. "I know Laura Madison would like to go. She works the bar at The Villa. You know Laura."

"Laura has a date," Larry said.

"Yeah, a date that can't dance." Greg scowled at Larry.

"Anybody else?" Greg grabbed another box from the back of Jackie's SUV.

"Well, I hear April Springer is available, and so is Susan Tatum. You might check with one of them."

Greg hummed to himself as he carried another box toward the house and Jackie reached in her SUV for another bag.

Jackie paused before walking by Larry. "I didn't realize you and Laura were dating now."

"We're not. I'm just taking her to the dance because she wants to go."

"I thought you were always working." Jackie passed by Larry, careful not to bump into his bandaged foot. The blacktop road edge turned to gravel and then grass but under the snow it was hard to know where to step.

"Not this year." Larry said looking straight ahead.

Jackie fought her instinct to smirk. Larry had never been free for any of her events when they dated. Every time she asked him to accompany her, he said he was working and after every event he accused her of flirting with other men in his absence. It was their most dividing issue.

"How nice for Laura." Jackie knew her voice might have had a sharp edge to it, but she fought hard to present a pleasant expression when she said it. Just as she pushed the bag to her left hip to pass by Larry, her boot heel hit the uneven edge of the blacktop and her ankle turned under her.

Larry reached forward and caught her just before she sat down in the snow. It happened so fast, the flash of pain in her ankle blended quickly into the humiliation of her clumsy exit. Jackie dropped the bagged pillow and Larry pulled her up to face him with his arms around her waist. "Are you hurt?"

"My ankle," Jackie said with a wince. "I may have sprained it." Jackie's arms were around Larry's neck and she rotated her ankle slowly.

"You may not be able to dance either."

It took Jackie a moment to process Larry's words and then she burst out laughing. "I'll let Laura dance with my date if you'll share your crutches."

Greg pushed through the storm door and ran down the steps. "What's going on out here? What's so funny?"

Larry squeezed Jackie's waist before pushing her away and smiled at Greg. "Jackie's throwing pillows at me."

Greg scowled and looked at Jackie.

"No, my heel hit the edge of the road and I turned my ankle. I dropped them." Jackie leaned over to pick them up off the ground, thankful Nolan had wrapped them in plastic.

"I'll get them. You just stay put." Greg grabbed another box and put the pillow on top to take back to the house. Betty waved from the door as she waited for Greg to get close so she could hold the door open for him.

Jackie turned to walk back for the last bag and felt a sharp pull when she put weight on her left foot. Walking gingerly on her toes, she limped to the side of her car.

"You need to go home and put some ice on that, so it doesn't swell. Keep it elevated." Larry regretted the words as soon as he said them. He knew Jackie always felt scolded and pushed back when he tried to give her unsolicited advice. He just couldn't help himself. It was an automatic reaction for him.

"I can't go home! I have a million things to do in the next two days."

Greg came outside again and gathered the last of Jackie's donations up without a word as Jackie shut her car doors. When he returned, Jackie walked between Larry's truck and her SUV to leave. "Thank you for your help. I'm sorry to take you away from your decorating. I know it will be beautiful tonight when it's finished. See you later, guys."

"Bye, Jackie." Greg returned Jackie's wave and stood facing Larry as Jackie pulled her car out onto the road. "She said she's got a date, but I still don't know who the guy is."

"It doesn't matter. Let's get this finished. We've still got to pick up a tree."

"I want to know who it is. Don't you?" Greg huffed.

"I guess we'll find out Saturday night."

CHAPTER TWELVE

Jackie rotated her ankle as she coasted into a parking space in front of Carlton Drugs. She didn't think the sprain was too bad, but she did need to put something on it. She was going to stop in there before heading to the mayor's office a block down the street.

Chester Hollis owned Carlton Drugs and he came around the corner as Jackie entered the store. "Hey, Jackie. Are you here to empty the box again?"

"No, Chester. I need one of those cold snap things you sell and a compression bandage. I've turned my ankle and I don't want it to swell."

"Oh, my. You need to rest and elevate it."

"Yeah, well, I don't have time for that. Do you have one of those cold things?"

"Sure, sure. Let me get it." Chester bustled off down an aisle and Jackie leaned on the counter with all her weight on her right foot. She probably needed to change shoes.

"Here you go," Chester said as he returned with both items and started to ring them up on the cash register. "I can put those things in a bag for you to take along. Maybe that will save you a trip later. There are some items in there that were bought here in the store as well as some clothes for Betty."

"Sure. I'll take them now while I'm here. I'll be running out there again. I just came from there. That's where I hurt my ankle."

"Are they doing okay?"

"I guess. As well as you can do when all this happens at Christmas. Larry and Greg Stanley are out there now putting up Christmas decorations for them."

"That's so nice."

"Yeah, it is." Jackie waited for Chester to gather the items up and wondered why she hadn't thought of it. She was not thinking straight lately. Decorating Betty's house should have been her idea. That was what she did, and she loved Christmas, but it hadn't even occurred to her.

Hobbling back to the car, Jackie decided she would drive down one block and park again. One block was a long way to walk right now. After this stop, she was going to change her footwear and do something about her ankle. She felt it swell at every beat of her heart.

"Hey, Donna." Jackie plopped down into a cushioned chair just inside the office door. "Sorry, but I have to sit. My ankle is hurting. Is the head honcho in?"

Donna smiled. "Yes, he's here."

"Can you ask him to come out here, please? The fewer steps I take, the better."

"Sure." Donna got up from her desk. "John, do you have a minute for Jackie?"

Jackie heard their muffled voices but was sure John didn't mind coming out to see her. John Talbot had recently become the new mayor of Carlton and he had been her brother's best friend in high school. She still had trouble seeing him as a public official because he had been the kid on her couch playing video games with her brother for years. She had made every effort to show him respect, however silly it seemed sometimes.

"Jackie, what's up?" John walked out into the lobby and looked down at her in the chair rubbing her ankle. "You've hurt yourself? I hope you didn't do it on city property." John chuckled nervously.

"No, I just twisted my ankle and I need to get off of it. The reason I'm here, well I had a thought..."

"Oh, no." John looked at Donna and smiled. "It's going to be one of those days."

Jackie knew he was teasing. He had been open minded about many of her ideas even if he hadn't always been brave enough to try them. "You know about the fire at the Parker's house?"

"I do. Sad--"

"Well, we have that silent auction planned for the Christmas dance. Now, I know it's a Chamber thing, not a city thing, and I'll run it by them too, but do you have any objections to making one of the silent auction items a donation to the Parkers?"

John looked over Jackie's head in thought for a moment. "I don't see any reason why not. The Chamber may not agree since they make money off the event, but the city shouldn't have any objection."

"But the city does run the vendor event on Saturday afternoon. Any problem with setting up a table with a collection jar on it for the Parkers there?"

"Ah, you see how she does," John said to Donna. "She distracts you with the first question to set you up for the second."

Jackie's mouth fell open and her eyes went wide as she feigned complete innocence of all allegations. "I am not so calculating as you make me out to be, Mayor Talbot."

"Yeah, I know. You forget. I know you." John chuckled as he pointed at Jackie and she smiled. "Go ahead. I don't have any objections to that either. Any other plots you want to unfold?"

"Nope. That's all I've got for you, but one thing for Donna."

Donna sat up straight and pointed at herself in question.

"The radio station needs the details on the city's plans for New Year's Eve. You know, times, places, etcetera. Can you email them to Missy at WBNC? She wants to put it on the air starting the 26th. I'm sure people are calling them to ask, and frankly I just don't have time today to get back with her. Would you do that for me?"

"Sure," Donna said with a dismissive wave. "I'll take care of it. You need to go take care of your ankle."

"I will. I'll hobble myself out of here." Jackie smiled as she stood, keeping her weight shifted to the left. "Oh, John. Do you know anywhere I could get some firewood? I thought the Parker's might need some. They are staying in Nolan Ramsey's house that's for sale on Maple Trail, and he hasn't lived there for over a year so there's no wood at the house."

"Do you see how she is?" John looked to Donna again and pointed at Jackie. "Did you drive around back before you came in here?"

"No," Jackie said. "Why would I do that?"

John shook his head. "My truck is back there with a flatbed attached to it. I just picked up a cord of wood."

"Really! Where did you get it?"

"South of town at the nursery."

"That's too far. I don't have time to drive down there. I thought maybe there was some here in town somewhere. I just wanted to get enough to give them some for the holidays, just for this week. I can't put that much in my car. I'll keep my eyes open. Thanks." Jackie hopped toward the door.

"Wait," John said. "Let me get the door. Pull your car around to the back and I'll give you some to take over there. I can spare a week's worth."

"Really! That would be great, John. I know they'll appreciate it."

"Yeah, yeah," John said as he shut the door behind Jackie and looked at Donna. "I swear that woman talks me out of something or into something every time she comes in."

"I think she did both this time!" Donna said. "But that's why we love her."

John smiled and pulled his keys from his pocket. "I'll be right back."

§

"You're going to drive all the way over there? Why? You don't need to see it. Just ask to see her books, her advertising, her business plan. What are you going to accomplish going all the way to Ohio?" Pamela threw her hands in the air and paced across the floor behind the couch.

"The boy is trying to be thorough." Ed Mackey sat in a leather-covered chair and Erik was on the couch facing the fireplace.

"What harm can it do to visit? I can make my pitch in person. I'm a lot more effective that way."

"You're personally involved with this woman," Pamela said to Erik. "Dad, it's going to be a mess. She's going to get mad at him when he breaks this thing off and she's going to want out. She won't want to work for him, and I'll end up having to referee. This will blow up in your face."

"Is that true, son? Are you involved with this woman?" Ed Mackey had been a vibrant, boisterous personality before his heart attack. The last few years he found the simplest things taxing, and limiting his involvement in the company was a goal he seemed unable to attain. His daughter had no flair for dealing with people and his son was clouded by ego. Perhaps both character flaws had been encouraged by Ed when he tried to keep his daughter away from clients and bolster his son's confidence. A budding personality was not to be manipulated.

"We're friends. That's all. Have I shown her some extra attention? Sure, I have. I wanted to find out what she had going. She likes me. I think she'll listen to me when I try to tell her how we can help her."

"And when she finds out that she's not the love of your life? Then what?" Pamela held up her hands. "You don't understand women, Erik. Women get mad and they hold grudges. Big grudges."

"Jackie is a businesswoman first. She has a good head on her shoulders. She won't think that joining our company means that she and I are joined. She's smarter than that."

"If that's true," Ed said softly, "I suggest you be honest with her about your future first. Then you make her an offer to join our company. That way her acceptance won't be linked in any way to your personal involvement. If you're not comfortable with that, you need to step back."

"You don't need to go visit." Pamela fell back in the chair across from her father.

"Really, Erik, that is going to intensify the whole situation. The gesture of you making a trip there personally to see her indicates a personal intimate interest. Any woman would read it that way. Get the data you need and make her an offer by phone without the visit. Then if she accepts, or she doesn't, you can visit all you want."

"I agree." Ed nodded. "Now, I'm going to rest until dinner."

Pamela jumped up to take her father's arm. His weakness worried her, and a future without him in it worried her even more. Pamela paused when his nurse stepped in to take his arm, and she sat in her father's chair.

"Look, Erik. We need to get on the same page here. If we're going to run this business together, we need to discuss this kind of thing."

"That's what we're doing right now."

"We're doing that because Dad needs an update. If Dad's involvement ends, I feel like you will stop communicating with me. We can't run a company together like that. We need to set down some guidelines and come to an agreement about--"

"Is that what you want to do? You want to run this business together?" Erik held up his hands in puzzlement. "I feel like I am always breaking my back to try and keep Mackey Enterprises going just like Dad did and you are trying to tear it down. I want to do this, and I want it to be successful. I don't think we're on the same page with that."

"We both want Dad to be happy." Pamela sighed.

"That may not be enough."

CHAPTER THIRTEEN

Jackie tapped her horn twice as she pulled in front of Larry's truck again at the Parker's temporary home. She couldn't imagine what he was still doing there. She had expected the Stanley brothers to be gone by now.

Greg flew out the front door and down the stairs two at a time to greet her. Before she could open her door, Jackie tapped the button to lower the driver's side window.

"Hey, Jackie. You're back!"

"Yes, I have firewood in the back now and I know Nolan has a lean-to built by the back door. I need to get this wood unloaded. Do you think I can drive back there? I don't want to tear up the yard or get stuck, but it's a long walk."

"I don't know if there's anything under the snow that would hurt if you did. Let me go inside and ask Tom. Just sit tight."

Jackie nodded and was happy to stay seated in her warm car. The sun was low in the sky now and she hoped to be home resting her foot within the hour. She needed to call The Villa and see if they wanted her to pick up donations there. It was too late to visit the post office, but she would do that early tomorrow. The karaoke machine! She'd forgotten to text Mitch about that. Her head was swimming. Would she get to sleep tonight?

"Hey," Greg said, popping up at her window again. "Tom said you can back up as far as that first window and then we'd have to carry from there. He's coming out back to help. You want to hop out and I'll drive it back?"

Jackie hesitated a moment, unwilling to stand up on her aching foot, but she really wasn't confident about backing her large SUV through the yard. Driving backwards was not her forte'. "Okay." Jackie grabbed her bag from the drugstore and relinquished her vehicle to Greg.

As soon as Greg pulled her car into the road to back in, Jackie saw Larry standing on the other side. "You want to sit here?" He motioned to the tailgate of his truck that she saw was littered with evergreen fragments. "It's getting pretty cold. You can get in the truck and I'll turn it on."

Jackie didn't answer. She began walking toward the passenger side of his truck, minimizing her limp as much as possible.

Larry crawled in the driver's seat and turned on the motor, leaving his crutches outside leaning against the truck. He put the heat on high and turned down the local country music radio station. "What's in the bag?"

"Ankle supplies from the drugstore. I've got a cold pack and a bandage."

"Put it on. You're going to be in a fix if that foot swells and you can't get your boot off."

Jackie hadn't thought about that. "I can't hop around right now. I need shoes on."

"Why?"

"Because I may have to go into The Villa when I leave here. Then I have to unload the karaoke machine from my backseat when I get home. I can't do any of that barefooted."

"Hmm," Larry said. "Well, how about I get your stuff from The Villa when we leave here, and you just hop into your house and get your snow boots on before you unload your car?"

"Okay. If you don't mind."

"I don't mind at all."

"Oh, I guess you were going by The Villa anyway. I wasn't thinking." Jackie leaned over and unzipped her boot. She immediately realized that pulling her heel loose from the shoe was going to hurt.

"Because of Laura? No. We're just friends. She told me that she's never been to the Harvest Ball or the Christmas party. She wants to go and for the first time I'm actually off work that night. I told her I'd take her. It's as simple as that."

"That's nice of you. I know she's told me before that she wanted to go, but when I offer to set her up with someone, she always declines."

"Well, my brother is not like that. Since we saw you earlier, he's already called and gotten himself a date."

Jackie chuckled. "Who did he call? April?"

"No, he called Nicole Samples. Do you remember her?" Larry unzipped his jacket.

"Is she really single? I thought she and Chad were just separated right now."

"That's all Greg is. He isn't divorced."

"He's not?" Jackie sat back. "Why is he so hot to trot about getting a date then?"

"He's not admitted it, but I think that's what got him separated to start with." Larry laughed when he saw Jackie's eyes widen with recognition.

"Shame on him!"

Larry shook his head. "The kid doesn't have any sense. He never did have." Larry looked down at Jackie's ankle. "You need to wrap it part of the way and then put the cold pack in..." Larry picked up the bandage. "Here, turn sideways with your back against the door and give me your foot."

Jackie started to protest, but she knew the determined scowl and ridged jawline meant Larry expected her to obey. Sometimes you had to pick your battles. "This is a little embarrassing." Jackie turned and put her left foot up.

"I don't know why. It's just a foot. I've seen your foot before."

Jackie looked away to pretend she wasn't in this awkward position and then realized she needed to pay attention so she could do this later. He wove the bandage around her heel, around her ankle and back again while inserting the cold pack before wrapping everything up.

"It will feel a little clunky to walk in, but it will keep it from swelling much more until you can elevate it."

"Thank you. It seems like I've been thanking you a lot lately."

Larry hummed and seemed uncomfortable with the praise. "So, who's the guy? Who are you seeing now?"

Jackie hesitated.

"I mean, if you don't mind me asking. I just wondered if it was someone I know."

"No, it's okay. He's not anyone you know. I met him when I was out of town--"

"Hey, Jackie." Greg banged on the window. "We're all done. I pulled your car back up."

"Thanks, Greg." Jackie just realized she had to hop to her car, and she looked in the side mirror to see how far away it was.

"You want to borrow one of my crutches?" Larry chuckled.

"To be honest with you, I'd probably sprain the other ankle trying to use crutches." She had never been very coordinated and always carried a concern that she might one day have to use crutches to get around. Just watching people use them was baffling to her.

"Wait. I'll move my truck up beside yours and you can just hop across."

Jackie nodded, but still tried to put her heel into her boots without success. As Larry backed up his truck to turn around, the Christmas lights came on all around the eaves of the house, the porch railing, and the stairs. Jackie gasped. "Look."

Larry glanced at the lights and saw Greg acting like a fool on the porch in an attempt to make Jackie laugh, but when he looked over at Jackie, she didn't seem to notice Greg at all. She was star-struck.

§

"Hey, Jackie. What are you up to today?" Calinda looked out the window of her wood shop and saw Nolan kicking up snow as he ran by with Scuba chasing him. "I figured you were probably too busy to stop by today. Is there anything you need for me to do?"

Calinda was not interested in attending any events that Jackie held, but she was always supportive of the hard work Jackie put in to make them all happen. She had endless errands to run and little help. Most of the year Calinda was buried in work, but the month of December was her relaxing time so the least she could do was try to give Jackie a hand.

"Nope, I'm all good. I'm just sitting in my living room floor in my pajamas playing with a karaoke machine."

"What? Doesn't that vendor thing start in about 3 hours? When does Erik get here?"

"Yesterday, I turned my ankle and it's killing me. So today, I took your advice and when I was talking with the principal about setting up the tables in the gym this morning, I asked him who was his student party planner. He gave me a name."

"Go back," Calinda said. "Did you go to a doctor? Is your ankle broken?"

"No. It can't be. I can move it. It just hurts to stand so I'm sure it's sprained. I'm trying to stay off of it."

"Okay, good idea. So, who is the little party planner?"

"A young man named Andrew Vick. He's a junior, and the principal told me he's a cheerleader."

"So, you called Maria?" Maria had been in school with Calinda and Jackie, but she was now the teacher that managed the high school cheerleaders.

"I did and she contacted Andrew for me, asking him if he wanted to help me out today. I was actually going to offer him some money, but Maria just asked him if he wanted to volunteer and he jumped at it. He came by the house and I gave him a list of errands to run for me while I figure out this crazy machine."

"So now you're sitting in the floor in your pajamas singing to the top forty tunes?" Calinda chuckled.

"I'm not that far yet, but I think I've got it hooked up right. I was just getting ready to test it. Do you have a special request?" Jackie laughed. "You know I can't sing."

"Me either. Do you need for me to pick up the donation boxes for you? I've got to run into town and then I'm going by to take Belly some Christmas cookies."

"Andrew has got that handled. He's probably already done that. I put that first on the list. He's just got a tiny car so he may have to make a few trips. I don't have to do anything except get dressed and go down to the high school gym. I'm going to sit down and put my foot up."

"Maybe you need some crutches." Calinda wondered if the drugstore had them.

"I can't manage that. I'll break my neck! I'm okay just hopping for now."

"So, you're going to a dance tonight and you can't dance?"

"Some sacrifice is always necessary. I'm being good during the day, so I can dance tonight." Jackie pulled herself up onto her couch and stretched her leg out.

"It doesn't work like that," Calinda shook her head. "It doesn't heal that fast."

"I'll worry about that tonight."

"Okay. Call me if you need me to come down there. What time is Erik due?"

"He said he'd call when he left Pittsburgh. He's got a lot going on there today, too. He has a brunch and then there are some evening events so he has to make sure everything is covered before he leaves town. I'd guess it will be late afternoon before he gets here."

"Are you getting nervous about his visit?"

Jackie hummed in thought. "I was yesterday. I was stressing a little about all the things I needed to do to be ready and worried about how he was going to see my town, my event. It's nothing like what he has in the city. For some reason today I'm only nervous about it being awkward. I tried to blend into his world, which wasn't hard, except for the French food. He has a glamorous life. I'm having a hard time imagining him blending into my Carlton life. I almost think he's not going to fit." Jackie hunched her shoulders. "We'll have to wait and see how it goes."

"He may be more down to earth than you realize. You saw him in a work environment. I'm sure he has a more casual mode and you just haven't known that side yet."

"He hasn't seen me at my own party yet either." Jackie laughed. "We may both be surprised!" Calinda agreed and Jackie promised to update her later.

It was possible Erik could relax, slump his shoulders, put up his feet and slurp the last of a milkshake from the cup, but Jackie couldn't imagine it. She couldn't imagine him changing a tire either. It had been silly of her to ever expect that he could.

CHAPTER FOURTEEN

"I did what you said, Jackie, and it worked perfect."   Andrew's enthusiasm was beginning to wear on Jackie as her ankle continued to throb with every heartbeat.

"Good. Is there anything to drink around here? I need to take a pill." Jackie was sitting on a barstool just inside the door to the gymnasium with her legs stretched out to rest on another stool positioned in front of her. "Here." She shoved her folded coat at Andrew and pointed to the barstool. "Can you put that over there?" When Andrew turned, she lifted her cowboy boot clad feet off the barstool and placed them back on top of her coat. Her heel was starting to hurt resting on the wood. "Thanks."

"There's water in the teacher's lounge. I'll go grab you a bottle."

"Good boy," Jackie muttered under her breath after Andrew ran off. "Callie girl!" Jackie almost forgot about her ankle and jumped to her feet when Calinda Ramsey walked in the door.

"Hey, Jackie. How is everything going?"

"Running smoothly. What's in the box?" Jackie pointed to a large box that Calinda carried in front of her.

"This is my donation for the silent auction." Calinda held it down so Jackie could see it.

"What is it?"

"It's a large salad bowl with matching smaller bowls." Calinda looked left and right. "Is he here yet?"

"Ah, that's why you brought this in! No, Erik hasn't left Pittsburgh yet. He's sent a few texts saying he is running here, running there, trying to leave by three o'clock. I don't know. I'm not holding my breath."

"You think he might not show?"

"He's been a little distant the last few times we've talked, and it's been awkward. I don't know what's going on, but yeah, I think he might just stand me up."

"Oh, no!"

"That's my life." Jackie tossed her hands in the air and slapped her palms down on her lap. Her intuition had been preparing her, and she found with each day that passed she cared less whether Erik showed up or not. The more they talked, the more she learned about his day-to-day life, his likes and dislikes, his dreams, the less she cared. He might have made a fascinating date, if only to spike the town gossip, but in the long run she knew they were ill-suited, and their futures went in different directions.

"I'm sorry about that, Jackie. You're not going to feel like dancing anyway. I'm glad you're keeping your foot up."

"Here you go." Andrew ran up with a bottle of water for Jackie.

"Hand me my purse please, will you?" Jackie pointed and Andrew fetched as he had been doing all afternoon. "Oh, Calinda, this is Andrew Vick."

"Hey." Andrew nodded, suddenly shy.

"Calinda Ramsey." Jackie completed her introduction and pointed to the tables on the side of the room. "You can take her auction item over to the display titled Willow Wood."

"Oh, you're the lady that makes the wood stuff?" Andrew pointed in surprise as Calinda nodded. "Wow! Nice to meet you."

"You, too." Calinda gave him the box and thanked him before he ran off. "Do you need anything? Do you need me to pick up the donation boxes?"

"Nope. Andrew has already done that. He's fielding things pretty well. I'm just supervising here. You know, I kind of like it this way."

Calinda laughed. "Does that mean you're going to keep limping?"

"Hello, ladies." Larry Stanley walked up behind Calinda.

"Hey, Larry. Did you bring goodies, too?" Calinda peered in the gift bag swinging from Larry's crutch.

"Ah, I did. The Sheriff sent me over here with a copy of his book for the auction.

"Have you read it?" Calinda and Jackie both looked at Larry as his eyes darted around the room.

"I think I'd like to exercise my constitutional right not to incriminate myself..."

Calinda laughed and patted him on the back. "Okay. I'll let you. I've got to get going. Jackie, call me if you need something. I'll talk to you later."

Jackie waved and then held her arm up high to catch Andrew's attention. "I've got a helper today. He'll be right over to get the book."

Larry looked curiously around the room for the helper and finally spotted the young man heading toward them. "He's a cheerleader, isn't he?"

"Yes. His name is Andrew Vick and the principal recommended him to me. So far he's working for free." Jackie elbowed Larry and winked, which made him chuckle.

"I've seen him at the games." Larry always supported his alma mater, the Carlton Cougars. "He's a high energy kid."

"I have to admit, I never knew how much I did until I had to describe every little detail to someone else. I need to raise my prices!" Jackie grinned as Andrew approached. "Another auction item from the Sheriff."

"Gotcha." Andrew ran off with Larry's bag.

Larry leaned against the door frame behind Jackie's shoulder and held his crutches out in front of him. "I guess this means your ankle is still hurting?"

"Yeah, I'm trying to stay off of it."

"You're not going to get much dancing done tonight." Larry smiled and looked down at Jackie's long legs in blue jeans perched on the barstool.

"More than you! How much longer are you going to be on crutches?"

"I go back to the doctor Monday. I hope I get to walk out of there. It's been over a month and he told me it should be off for Christmas if everything went well."

"I'm expecting to be completely healed any minute now!" Jackie chuckled. "But I'm not going to tell Andrew."

Larry laughed. "There are perks! They benched me to a desk for almost a month and that drove me crazy, but not being able to climb up on Tom Parker's roof the other day didn't bother me at all. Greg needs to do something useful."

"Hey, Jackie." Andrew panted slightly from his run across the gym. "A lady named Deandre is here with appetizers. She's got about ten boxes in her car and she's parked behind Mr. Kenny's shop class. What do you want me to do?"

"Go to the office and get the red wheeled cart behind Donna's desk and use that to unload everything to Mrs. Johnson's classroom. Then open that yellow box we put in there. It has large gold platters and the small red box has white paper lacy doilies, round paper sheets that you put on the plates first. Then you place the food on the paper. If they are small bite-size appetizers, put them out in a circular pattern and then pyramid them up."

Andrew nodded.

"You might want to set up the punch bowls while you're at it. Shirley will be here soon with the punch."

"I'm on it!" Andrew sped off across the gym.

"I want him to come work free for me next." Larry huffed.

"Hey! You're going to have to take a number."

They quietly watched the hustle and bustle of townspeople visiting the exhibits set out for the businesses. The hallway was lined with booths for the local retail owners to show their services and products. The proceeds of the dance helped fund the Carlton Chamber of Commerce and the small businesses in Carlton.

"Not to dredge up the unfortunate past," Larry said, cautiously. "But I parked beside you outside and you still don't have a license plate on your car. I'm not nagging--" Larry held up his hands in self-defense when Jackie turned sharply in her seat.

"I do! I do have a tag. It's in my back seat!"

"Okay, good. Any reason why you're keeping it there?"

"Because I haven't had time to go find a screwdriver. I know I have one somewhere, but I never think of it when I'm home. Those people down at the BMV didn't even offer to put it on for me. Can you imagine?"

Larry smiled. "Well, that's not really in their job description, I guess. Would you like for me to go put it on? I've got a screwdriver in my truck."

Jackie hesitated. "No. No, that's okay. I can do it. I'll try to remember and do it tomorrow." Her car was locked, and Jackie didn't want to make him hobble all the way back into the school to return her car keys.

Larry chuckled. "Okay. Well, I'll see you later." Reaching to position his crutches, he lightly pinched Jackie's cheek. "Take it easy, boss."

"I will." Jackie looked over her shoulder and watched Larry swing through the lobby on his crutches with ease.

§

By six o'clock, Jackie knew that she was going to be without a date for Christmas again. Erik had called and sent texts a few times throughout the day to continue his saga of how busy he was. Well, she was busy too! She had an entire dance to put on by herself. Except for Andrew's willingness to help, the whole event was on her shoulders. He was just overseeing dozens of other people. It was not the same thing.

Dancing was out of the question. Sadly, Jackie changed her plans for her evening attire. The red dress was too long for flat shoes and she knew she needed to be as comfortable as possible. Andrew would not be there to manage the evening for her. Instead she wore a sparkling aqua and silver dress with flat silver ballet slippers that accommodated her meticulously wrapped ankle. A sensible choice, but it lacked the holiday feel.

As she rushed out her door, she answered her phone when she saw it was Calinda calling. "Hey, Callie!"

"Hi. Are you at the gym?"

"No, just walking out my door and headed that way. I had to run home and change. I left Andrew there to keep an eye on things, but he's going to leave once I get back."

"So? Any more word from Erik?"

"Just more texts. He's not said it, but I know he's not coming. I don't even care right now. I'm tired. My ankle hurts. I haven't eaten all day, and I'm not up to entertaining someone who will probably think my town is a big joke." Jackie slammed her car door. "I'm just fed up!"

Calinda giggled. "Tell me how you really feel."

"I know. It's time to put my party face on."

"You'll be fine once you get there."

"You're probably right. I'll get busy and it will be over in a blink. Then I'll rest for a couple of days. Are you sure you and Nolan won't stop in? I'll leave some tickets at the door for you."

"No, thank you. Nolan dislikes these things almost as much as I do. We have the fire built up high and plan to snuggle on the couch to watch a movie."

"I'll fill you in tomorrow, but you're going to miss out on some wonderful pageantry, and you'll never believe me when I try to describe it to you."

Calinda giggled. "I'll take that risk. Take it easy, but try to have fun."

"You, too."

"I'm sorry Erik isn't living up to your expectations. I know you thought he was the perfect guy."

"He seemed to have all the right qualities, but it was all superficial. Even from the start I knew it couldn't work. It just wasn't right and I definitely couldn't ever marry him. I told you what his last name was, right? I can't have people calling me Jackie Mackey!"

Calinda was laughing when she said goodbye.

CHAPTER FIFTEEN

Jackie parked her car at the corner of the building. She would need the overhead light when she closed up. Locking up and leaving was usually the worst part of these events. Being the last person there at the end of an evening was like the day after Christmas. Tonight though, she might be ready for it to end.

Walking into the gym, everything looked set up perfectly and the band was in the back carrying in their equipment. She checked the tables and rearranged a couple of things before heading to the cafeteria.

"Hey, Jackie." Andrew met her in the hallway as he pushed the red cart loaded with supplies for the table.

"Hey, Andrew. You can go now. I'll take it from here. I appreciate all of your help today."

"Uh, okay. Are you sure? I can stay if you want."

"No, that's okay. There's not much to do this evening. When everything is set up correctly, the events run pretty smooth."

"It was fun. I'm glad you called me. Call me anytime. I'm happy to help."

"Do you mean that? Is this really something you'd like to do? I know you have school stuff."

"Yeah, there are the games, but other than that, I'm free. I love helping set up parties. You have the coolest job."

"Well, if it's something you think you'd like to do, you can come work for me." She didn't want Andrew to graduate and open his own party business. Better to keep him on her side and not have him working against her.

"That would be great! Thanks."

"Have a good evening." Jackie waved and turned to push the cart back to the gym.

"Geeze, these kids are messy!" Sandy picked up a plastic bucket and scraped crumbs off the table.

"That table over by the door is covered in melted ice cream and it's sticky." Mitch straightened the chairs under the table.

"The kids had a ball, though." Sandy chuckled. "I loved that elf game you played. I laughed as much as they did."

"Yeah, it's a fun age. The boys can get a little rowdy, but at least we didn't have teenagers!"

Sandy nodded. "Did you hear from Erik today?"

"I haven't, but I assume he's in Ohio."

"After church tomorrow, we need to call Jackie." Sandy gave Mitch a knowing glance. "I'm going to call Jackie. You don't have to get involved. I'll tell her."

"No, I agree. We'll tell her together. You know, she may still do it. She may be dazzled by Erik's offer. He's really good at what he does, and we can't be disappointed if she decides to take the offer."

"I know, but we won't be able to live with ourselves if we don't do what we can to give her the information she needs to make that decision."

Mitch nodded. "I did hear from Cindy today. She called while the kids were eating."

"Cindy from Murrysville?"

"Yeah, she was calling to ask if we had a folding dolly that could move more than three hundred pounds, but we got to talking. She said she went to an event Friday night and Pamela was there."

"Really? I didn't think she ever attended Mackey events." Sandy tied up her black plastic garbage bag and tossed it by the door.

"I didn't think so either, but she said Pamela is frustrated with Erik. She said he doesn't have the business sense needed to run the company, but she wishes he did because she'd like to leave."

"Leave? Where is she going?"

"I don't know. I guess she doesn't like it, but she told Cindy that her dad wasn't doing well. He barely had the energy to move from the table to the chair. Some decisions are going to have to happen. They can't both run the company. One of them has to be in charge."

"I don't like either choice."

"I feel the same way," Mitch said as he loaded the serving dishes into a plastic tote to take home. "It's going to be a power struggle and I'm afraid we'll suffer the most."

"Maybe I should look for a job again. I haven't been looking and I might be able to find something part-time that will still leave me available to help you out on evenings and weekends. Once the holidays are over, I'll see what I can find."

"I think this next year will be my last one with Mackey. I'm not going to tell Erik that, but that's my goal."

"Then we can move to Ohio so I can keep an eye on Mom."

"Maybe Jackie will hire me on as her helper." Mitch chuckled.

"That just might work out!"

§

Jackie had been hiding in the cafeteria long enough and it was time to face the remains of the high school gym. It was midnight, the band was gone and most of the people had filed out to their cars. Music still played and food was still on the tables, so she needed to go see how much damage had been done. The table cloths had to be gathered, the food and drink removed, and the tables straightened up enough to leave overnight. She had hired cleaners to come in early tomorrow.

As she made the turn in the hallway, she saw Larry leaning against a row of lockers. He had replaced his suit jacket with his Sheriff's office coat, but he still had the tie on from the dance. She had spoken to Laura and Larry earlier in the evening. They were at a larger table with some of Larry's coworkers from the Sheriff's office. His brother, Greg, had been dancing much of the evening, but left early with his date. He seemed to enjoy the band.

"Hey, I thought you were gone." Jackie tried hard not to limp, but she had been up on her feet too long.

"I took Laura home about an hour ago, but I just came back."

Jackie's forehead furrowed. She couldn't imagine why he would come back unless he was looking for Greg. "Greg left hours ago."

"I know, but I just thought I'd hang around until everyone cleared out."

"Oh, you don't have to do that. I'm just going to pick up a little before I lock up. I'm going back in there to shut down the music now, so the last few people will know that they need to clear out."

"I don't want you to lock up by yourself. I'll stay until you're done."

"Larry," Jackie said with an unconscious eye roll. "I always lock up by myself."

"No. It may seem that way to you, but I'm always out there. You may not see me, but I'm around. I'm usually working."

Jackie felt her throat tighten to ward off tears. She must be really tired if something as simple as that would make her cry. Larry probably just felt like he was doing his job. "Well, I'll just be a few minutes."

Turning to walk by him, Larry reached out and took her hand. "You haven't even had a dance tonight."

Jackie smiled. "I'm in no shape to dance and neither are you."

Larry leaned his crutches on the locker doors and pulled her toward him. "We are in the best shape together. We are two right feet, not two left feet."

Jackie smiled as she fell easily into his arms. Neither did more than sway from side to side without shifting their weight, but Jackie felt his cheek press against her temple. It was a safe place. They had dated off and on for over two years, so it was comfortable being in his arms. She was glad they had finally found a friendship and the hurt had begun to mend.

CHAPTER SIXTEEN

Sunday morning, Jackie grabbed her laptop and limped to her living room couch. Snuggling under her favorite purple afghan, she propped the laptop open and settled in to pay some bills. She had paid the band last night, but the table and chair rentals, the cleaning service, and the caterers still needed her attention. After this, she had nothing on her agenda except rest. She had three days with no events, and she planned to heal her ankle with positive thoughts.

When her cell phone rang and she saw it was Erik calling, she hesitated. It was too soon to talk to him. She resented the fact he had disregarded his commitment to her but wasn't that what Larry had always complained about. He had never understood that an event planner had to put her business first over her personal plans. It was very hypocritical of her if she couldn't be understanding of Erik's obligations to his business now.

Reluctantly, she answered the call.

"Good morning, sunshine! So, tell me all about it. How did it go last night? I hate that I missed it. I really wanted to be there, but I want to hear all about it."

"Oh, there's nothing much to tell. I do it every year and it went just as expected. You didn't miss much."

"Of course, I did. I missed you! I wanted to be there. I want you to know that. It's just Christmas is really a stretch for us. All of the staff have to give a hundred percent for us to meet all of our obligations. When one worker gets sick or runs late, the whole structure falls apart and I have to pitch in wherever I'm needed. You know how it is."

"I understand."

"So, is your ankle feeling better? I don't know how you pulled all of this off by yourself with a sprained ankle. You're an amazing woman, Jackie Knight!"

"I had help. I found a student from the high school to work with me during the day and so I was able to stay off my feet. That made the evening bearable. He's a good kid and I'm glad I found him. I'll use him again."

"That's super! Your expansion has already begun. Are you going to start cultivating jobs in the nearby towns after the first of the year?"

"I'll look into it in January. Right now, I'm just focused on finishing this year."

"Don't I know it! It's been an exhausting year. My company has gone through so many changes. I think this next year will be the start of different times for us. We've been talking about expanding our reach, just like you. We'd like to find other companies that are looking for support and offer them a helping hand by coming under the umbrella of Mackey Enterprises. That way we can offer them guidance, training, supplies and general business support that presents such a struggle to small business owners. I've talked to my board about Knight Events."

"You have?" Jackie leaned back on her pillow with a furrowed brow. "What about Knight Events?"

"Well, I gave my board general information about your business and what your goals are for growing your company. They're intrigued by your location and think you would be an excellent candidate for expansion with Mackey Enterprises. If you joined our company, we would be there for you when you sprained your ankle or to pitch in if you had more events than you could handle alone. We have advertising dollars that we could throw your way and help you get a foothold into those small towns situated around Carlton. We could help you pull all that business in and then manage the personnel that you hired. We have a topnotch human resource department and payroll provider. That would take all of that financial management chore off your plate!"

Jackie chuckled. "That's actually what I'm sitting here doing right now. I need to pay the people from the event last night."

"See what I mean? We would do all that for you. What do you think? Does it sound like the kind of help you could use?"

"Yeah, sure it does. I hate the finances, and I can't find any more hours in the day to pursue business in other towns. I could definitely use help--"

"That's great! Just send us your financials for the last two years, and I'll have my board look it over so they can make you an offer. I'm really excited about us working together. It will be--"

"I would be an employee of Mackey Enterprises?" Jackie's eyebrows shot up and her back stiffened.

"Yeah, we would be a real team."

"No. No, thank you. I'm not interested in being anything more than Knight Events. All that you offer sounds tempting, but that's just not the direction I'm looking to go."

"Don't make a rash judgment. Let the board give you a formal offer. I think you might be surprised at the value of the business you've built. You'll still get to run it as you see fit. We would just be there to help--"

"I appreciate it. Really I do, Erik, but I'm not interested. Oh, I've got someone at my door. I need to go. We'll talk another time. You have a good day."

"You, too. Get some rest. I'll call--"

Jackie disconnected the phone. There was no one at her door, but she'd already made it clear to Mitch that she wasn't interested in being bought out. Although he hadn't complained at all, she could sense that Mitch was not happy in the arrangement he had with Erik's company. Mitch was in a different place in his career and it might have made sense for him, but Jackie considered it a sign of failure to let someone buy her company. She wasn't ready to give up on it yet and she wasn't sure she could work for someone else. She preferred doing things her own way.

Jackie finished up her bills and moved her laptop to the coffee table. Picking up her cell phone, she checked the time to make sure she wasn't calling during the lunch hour and dialed the phone number for Mitch. She had promised to let him know about the karaoke machine anyway, and she'd see what Mitch's reaction was to Erik's offer.

"Hi, Sandy! It's Jackie Knight. I hope I'm not calling at a bad time."

"Hello, Jackie. No, it's a great time. How have you been?"

"Well, I'm still limping around a little with a sprained ankle, but my big Christmas party is over, so I'll get a few days of rest now. Did all of your weekend events go well?"

"Yes, everything has gone very nicely. We have a small church group tonight and that will wrap it all up for us."

"Well, I was just calling to tell Mitch about the karaoke machine."

"Oh, he's right here. Let me get him."

"Jackie? Hey! I was going to call you this afternoon."

"Hi, Mitch. I wanted to let you know that I got the karaoke machine home and I think I've figured out how to hook it up. I can't really test it here, so I can't promise I won't have a problem on Christmas Eve."

"If you do, just give me a call. I don't mind at all. I'll just be here at home."

"I appreciate that."

"I was going to give you a call today to see how things went with your party and with Erik's visit."

"Oh, you didn't hear? Erik never showed up. He spent all day promising he was coming and then when it was too late, he called to say he was detained. Apparently, there was a party that had a staffing shortage somewhere and he had to step in--"

"Step in?" Mitch cackled and held his hand over the receiver, but Jackie could hear him tell Sandy her story. "I'm sorry, Jackie, but Erik doesn't step in. He might have been giving directions or orders, but he wouldn't actually do anything. I don't know if he's ever even held a single event on his own."

"Hmm."

"Now don't get me wrong," Mitch said, clearing his throat. "I'm not trying to speak ill of him; it's just not his thing. He's a coordinator but at a high level."

"I understand what you're saying. I talked to him again this morning and he asked me to provide my financial records to his board. He thinks that Mackey Enterprises might be able to help me."

"Really?" Mitch repeated Jackie's words to Sandy in the background. "If you don't mind, can I put you on speaker? Sandy wants to join us."

"Sure! The more the merrier." Jackie had liked Sandy the instant they had been introduced. She had pulled into the parking garage and parked beside her car while the mechanic from the towing company was changing the tire. Sandy had hopped out of the car and embraced Jackie in greeting as if they were old friends.

"Jackie," Sandy said. "Before you make any decisions about Mackey Enterprises, I'd like to tell you how it has been for us. Not to say your experience will be the same way, but I don't want you to make any commitments without hearing our story."

"Oh, I've already given Erik my answer, but I suppose I still have the opportunity to change my mind. I'll warn you though, I'm pretty hard-headed, and it's not easy to talk me out of things."

Jackie heard Mitch chuckle before Sandy continued. "We were looking for a helping hand. We were working night and day, but barely making ends meet. We couldn't expand, but we couldn't retire. Erik's offer seemed like a golden opportunity for us to finish out our career with less stress."

Jackie hummed in agreement.

"Unfortunately, nothing we expected has ever happened. We work with no payroll for materials and we are never offered any funds to hire even part-time help. We aren't given adequate decorations, dinnerware, or music, so those purchases have come from our own pockets. We work harder now than we did before Mackey Enterprises and we get less pay. Erik makes promises that he just doesn't keep, and his sister, Pamela, is rude and insulting. Oh, Jackie, if we ever had the opportunity to go back in time, we would never have signed those papers. Please, give this some serious thought before you—"

"Oh, I turned Erik down flat. I'm not sending my financials anywhere, and I'm not working for Mackey Enterprises. You don't have to worry a minute about that."

Sandy laughed and clapped her hands.

"Again, I don't want to speak ill of my employer," Mitch said. "But I like you, Jackie. We like you, and we want you to be happy and successful. I don't think you would be, working for Mackey Enterprises."

"I thought you might say that. I could sense that about you when we were at the conference."

"Well, you are very astute!" Sandy called out gleefully.

"Do you think that's why Erik paid me so much attention? Was it all just about the company?"

"Oh, I think he was genuinely smitten with you," Mitch said.

"He didn't try to court us when he made us an offer." Sandy chuckled. "Did he, Mitch?"

"Nope. He was pretty smooth though. He's more salesman than event planner, but maybe that's the role the company made him play."

"Well, I won't keep you both any longer and I appreciate your concern about me, but you have nothing to worry about."

"Oh, good."

"Unless I can't get the karaoke machine to work Thursday, and then you'll be hearing from me." Jackie laughed along with Mitch and Sandy before saying goodbye. As it turned out, the conference in Pittsburg had been beneficial to her, because she had made good friends with two people who were knowledgeable and genuinely kind. That didn't happen every day.

CHAPTER SEVENTEEN

Thursday was Christmas Eve and Jackie was well rested. Except for an occasional twinge, her ankle was healed, and she pulled on her snow boots, throwing a second pair of comfortable shoes in a bag. A couple of additional inches of snow had fallen on Tuesday and she needed to load the karaoke machine back into her car.

Pulling up to the Stanley's farmhouse, she saw Greg on the porch, and the furniture truck already backed up to the front of the house. She had rented long banquet tables for the dinner, but first they had to remove some of the furniture from Barbara's house to make room. Jackie found the man in charge and relayed her instructions while she walked him around the living room.

Greg helped by holding the front door open, and soon the caterers arrived to set up the kitchen. Family began arriving shortly after one o'clock, and the Stanley house became chaotic with Barbara's grandchildren running around the table as their mothers chased them down. Jackie assigned the karaoke machine to Greg since his mother said he was mechanically inclined and he began to work on the connections, testing the sound when he wanted attention.

By mid-afternoon all of Barbara's children and their families had arrived except for Larry. Jackie hadn't seen him all day. When Barbara's sister arrived with all of her family, she began to think Larry had decided to stay away today. She hoped it was not because she was there.

"Jackie, you remember my sister, Deloris?"

"I do. How are you? Merry Christmas!" Jackie leaned in when Deloris held her arms open for a hug.

"Merry Christmas, dear. I was a little worried when it snowed again, but it's a beautiful day out there and the roads are all clear."

"Oh, Deloris, did I tell you about Betty?" Barbara handed Deloris a paper plate and pointed at the cookie and fudge display on the counter. "She had a house fire. She and Tom lost almost everything. I invited them to come over today, but they said they have kids coming home.   They're staying in another house that's for sale on Maple Trail."

"That's terrible. They probably lost all of their gifts, too. I hope their whole Christmas isn't ruined."

"They're doing okay," Larry said as he stepped up behind Barbara and startled her. "I just stopped by and saw them this morning."

"Well, where did you come from?" Barbara chuckled.

"Hey Aunt Deloris." Larry took the coats that Jackie was holding and brushed by her to take them to the back room.

"Where has that boy been?" Deloris asked Barbara.

"I don't know," Barbara shrugged. "Probably working. He's been a caged animal for the last few weeks because he was on crutches. I'm so glad they took those away."

"When I stopped by the Parkers this morning, they told me Jackie had been by," Larry said as he walked back in the kitchen. Moving behind Jackie, he squeezed her shoulders. "Said she brought them a nice sum of money she collected."

Jackie shook her head. "No, it was a collection from the Chamber Christmas party. I dropped it off Monday."

"That was nice of you, dear." Deloris pinched a piece of fudge off her plate and took a small bite. Fudge was her holiday weakness.

"Not just nice; he said it was almost fifteen hundred dollars!" Larry laughed. "I told Tom he was more popular than I thought."

"How did you do that, Jackie?" Barbara patted Jackie's hand.

"I didn't do anything. It was just donations that were left at the party."

"You put up a box and sign, didn't you? You put it on the auction table." Larry pointed at Jackie and nodded. "That's where it came from."

"Yes. I hope it helps them. It won't rebuild a house, but maybe it will replace the lost gifts."

"I would bet just knowing the town is thinking of them is enough to save Christmas for their family."

"Everyone has been very generous." Jackie quietly backed away from the kitchen, so the sisters could chat, and checked on the kids in the living room. Greg was playing with the light strip that came with the karaoke screen and his nephew was peering intently at the instruction manual from the box. Larry appeared at her back again with his hands on her shoulders and whispered in her ear. "If you'll give me your car keys, I'll go put your license plate on your car."

Jackie turned around and glared at Larry. "You are never going to be at peace until that's done, are you?"

Larry laughed demurely. "I guess not. Every time I see it, all I can think about is that it needs to be fixed."

"Okay. Okay, I'll get them. My purse is in the bedroom."

Returning with the keys, she handed them to Larry, and he held her fingers for just an instant longer than seemed necessary before heading out the front door. His left foot was encased in a black boot that kept him from having a normal stride, but he was bearing weight on his foot. Jackie looked out the living room window and watched him crouch down at the back of her SUV. When he began walking around her car and scrutinizing the tires, she walked outside.

"Is something wrong?"

"No, I'm just checking out the tire they put on. You really should get another new tire and have them all rotated."

"Why?"

"Because the tread is uneven. You have one new tire and three old ones."

"Pfft, it's fine." Jackie walked up and looked at the tires. "I'm not going any long distance. I have to take the karaoke machine back to Barnesville Monday, but other than that, I'll just be here in town."

"No more trips to the city?"

Larry's cold glare caused Jackie to hesitate before responding. "No."

"So, the guy," Larry said as he walked around her car toward her. "The guy that was supposed to come to the Christmas party, is that over?"

Jackie squinted her eyes and held her tongue. Her gut reaction was to tell him that it was none of his business, but if they were going to be friends, there was nothing wrong with him asking. Living in Carlton, Ohio, he would find out anyway. "Yes, that's over."

Larry just nodded and looked down at his feet. "I can dance a little better now." Holding up his booted foot, he smiled.

"Well, if Greg gets the music working, you might get the chance." Rubbing her arms, she turned to walk back in the house and Larry followed, grabbing her hand to press her keys into her palm.

"Thank you for putting the plate on for me. Now that everything is all fixed, you can rest easy."

Larry hummed and reached around Jackie to pull the door open for her. "I don't think everything is quite right yet."

Jackie looked over her shoulder with a puzzled frown, but before she could ask Larry for clarification, his mother called to her from the kitchen.

"Jackie, I want to put the potatoes in that oval dish, the one with the scalloped edge. Have you seen it? It's not on the counter. Maybe one of my boys put it up in the top cabinet. I never put anything up there because I can't reach it, but they always seem to think it's the perfect place for everything." Barbara bustled around the kitchen opening every cabinet and looking inside.

"The caterers brought serving dishes. We can just use what they--"

"No. No, I want that dish on the table. It's my mother's platter and I always use it every holiday."

"Let me get the step stool from the utility room and I'll look up in that top cabinet." Jackie had seen the step stool folded and resting next to the washing machine. She had used it herself last year when she needed to reach the cabinet over the refrigerator. The top cabinet that Barbara suspected the boys were using for her occasional dishes was a large lift-up door above her top kitchen cabinets. At first she had thought it was just a decorative touch in place of the ordinary soffits, but Barbara had explained that her husband, Lawrence had used it to store camping supplies and items he didn't want the children to touch. Once she climbed up the steps and peered in, she found seldom used kitchen appliances, old toys, and games, along with some camping cookware. "Not in here. Let me check the other side."

Jackie repeated her actions on the other side of the room and was successful. Holding up the long platter, Barbara cheered.

"That's it! You found it. What in the world was it doing over there? Those boys--"

"What are you blaming on me now?" Greg swung around the corner grinning and looked up at Jackie. "You're going to break your neck up there. Here." Greg took the platter from Jackie and passed it to his mother. "Be careful. That second step wobbles sometimes. You need to throw this ladder away, Mom. I'll get you a new one down at the hardware store. That thing is older than I am!"

Larry stood in the doorway watching his brother, Greg, take Jackie's hand and put his arm around her waist as she came backwards down the ladder. He couldn't justify the frustration that swelled inside of him. His brother was a flirt. He always had been, and he knew Jackie merely tolerated Greg. There was nothing there that should have any effect on him, yet every time something like that happened, he lost his head. It was one of the main reasons his relationship with Jackie had ended months ago. He accused her of flirting with other men when she was at her parties and events. She had tried to tell him that it was all just work, just a part of being friendly and managing the events. He was the one that couldn't manage the events. He didn't like sharing her with the whole town.

Jackie turned around and stepped aside as Greg folded the step stool up to return it to the utility room for her. Jackie's eyes locked on Larry's and she saw the familiar transformation come across his face. He was angry. Larry had always struggled with accepting his brother's personality. They were very different, and Larry thought Greg was inconsiderate and immature. With Greg living out of state, the challenges were fewer, but unfortunately, their camaraderie was sometimes forced.

Larry turned without a word and disappeared from the doorway as Barbara called out to one of the wait staff to help her with the potatoes. Jackie surveyed the kitchen and felt they were close to mealtime. Everything seemed on schedule and she was afraid Larry would drive off. His usual way of managing his feelings was to run from them. She slipped quietly from the kitchen, grabbed her coat, and stepped out on the front porch.

Larry's truck was still parked on the side of the road and he wasn't inside. Looking down at the footprints in the snow, she saw they led toward the horse barn and she followed them. She felt certain this could be easily resolved and then Christmas could proceed as intended. Being Larry's friend was turning out to be harder than she had anticipated.

CHAPTER EIGHTEEN

Larry walked in the barn and took a deep breath. Just being outside was calming to him, but the barn held a special comfort. The Stanley Farm had always kept horses among many other animals, but Larry's earliest memories were of being in this barn with his father. His father had always worked off his anger. Every scolding Larry had received had been from his father while he worked. He would be hammering the fence or cleaning out the stalls while he reprimanded him. He wasn't one for staring a person down. That was his mother's trick. She would hold her children captive with her targeted gaze and perhaps a pointed finger in their face.

Larry smiled as he stroked the nose of a boarded mare named Walnut. He had learned to manage his anger by removing himself from the situation. Closing doors to negativity kept him looking forward. He had always been able to leave behind anything that wasn't good for him. Jackie was that one exception.

Even when he stayed away from her for months, she was in the back of his mind and his eyes were always searching for her. Rationally, he knew she hadn't done anything to encourage Greg and he knew Greg was just being himself. The combination, however, was explosive to him.

"Hello there." Jackie stepped inside the barn and approached Larry slowly. "What are you doing?"

"Just came outside for some air."

"Well, the air in here doesn't smell all that great." Jackie pinched her nose and made a face until Larry laughed.

"Maybe not, but it's my second home. I'm used to it. What are you doing out here?"

"Looking for you." For a long moment all they did was stare at each other. "Are you okay?" Jackie stepped closer and reached out to touch Walnut's nose.

Larry's throat was tight, and he didn't respond. He watched Jackie touch Walnut's cheek timidly. He remembered her fear the first time she had been in his family's barn. She had wanted nothing to do with the horses, but over time she had won them over, too. She would come out to the barn and talk to him while he worked as the horses called to her for attention. They seemed entertained by her presence.

"Is Greg getting on your nerves? You know he's just a big goof. He can't help it." Jackie rolled her eyes and shook her head. "I'm sure he won't stay much longer. As soon as he works out his home situation, he'll be gone."

"Yeah, I know. That's why I just need to walk away when he gets on my nerves."

"A good plan. We don't need any fights on Christmas. Dinner will probably be ready in about thirty minutes and your mom will be looking for you." Jackie stepped back to turn, and Larry reached for her hand.

Pulling her into an embrace, Larry kissed her cheek. "I'm glad you're here."

Jackie stepped back and nodded. "I'll see you inside." Waving as she pushed the barn door shut, Jackie tried to find her footsteps in the snow, so she could step back into them. Larry was acting strangely, and she didn't know what more she could do for him. He seemed okay now that he was outside and hopefully he would return without any animosity toward Greg, but if she had learned one thing in all her event planning engagements, she had learned that family dynamics were a complicated thing.

§

The dinner went smoothly from the kitchen where Jackie sat, hiding away out of sight. The diners seemed cheerful and the children well behaved. Jackie began overseeing the cleanup before the meal ended and directed the caterers on storing the excess. Once the family moved out of the dining area, Jackie slipped in and removed all the tablecloths to shove into plastic bags for later, straightening chairs as she went by.

When she heard Greg begin tampering with the karaoke machine, she knew it was time to escape.

"I'm going to head home now," Jackie whispered in Barbara's ear as she leaned down to Barbara's chair. "The kitchen is all cleaned up. Leftovers are stored in the fridge for tomorrow. You send me a text when you are ready for the furniture movers to come back to pick up the tables and I'll send them over."

Barbara patted her arm. "Thank you, Jackie, and Merry Christmas."

"Merry Christmas, Barb."

Jackie was pleased with her quiet departure and opened the back of her SUV to toss in the tablecloths. Now that the sun was down, the colder temperatures added a crisp layer to the top of the snow and each step she took made a crunching sound. Before closing the back door, she reached in her pocket for her gloves and slipped them on.

It had been a long day and she felt a sudden melancholy knowing it was her last event of the calendar year. She was going to take this next week to do some event planning for herself. She was going to construct a plan to advertise and reach out to the towns within the county. Spring would be coming soon and there would be lots of opportunity to hold special sales, events and celebrations. When school was out, Andrew might be free to work regularly for her during the summer months, and she would cultivate part-time hires in the neighboring towns, too. It was time she focused on her professional life instead of her personal life. It seemed to be the one thing she could count on.

When she reached the main street of Carlton, she took the main road and drove by the decorated shops. The church had a lighted display on the lawn, and the town's decorations lighted each pole with a candy cane or Christmas tree. The Villa was still open, and their windows were draped with small twinkling lights that danced on the banked snow piles lining the streets.

Jackie didn't have a Christmas tree. She always thought she would get one, but the holiday season never seemed to allow for it. It was not just a busy time; it was a time for everyone else. Her events were always her first concern, and her focus was on providing the holiday spirit for others. Somehow there was never enough time for her to have a Christmas for herself.

Driving around the block, she headed down her street, but slowed her car as she neared her little white house and leaned forward against the steering wheel to look up. Christmas lights were wrapped and twisted all around her porch columns with blinking lights stretched across the front eaves of her porch. A fresh Christmas tree leaned to one side at the end of the porch with lights and garland wrapped among the snowy branches. Throwing the car into Park, she jumped out and leaned back against the driver's door to stare at it. It was breathtaking. Sure, there were other houses on the block with lights and decorations, but this was her house. How did this happen?

A vehicle pulled up behind Jackie's car and she squinted into the headlights. When the light went out, Larry stepped out of his truck and walked toward her.

"Did you do this?"

"Do you like it?" Larry didn't want to be charged with vandalism, so he decided to tread lightly.

For a long moment Jackie just stared at her house and step-by-step Larry came closer until he was only inches away. Six months ago he had promised himself that he would not pursue Jackie Knight again. He had been hurt and exhausted from the emotional roller coaster that her events and her lifestyle were causing him. Even though he reminded himself of that often, he had never been able to stop wishing that she would come back to him. The heartache at hearing she was seeing someone new made him realize that he had only one option. He needed to tell her how he felt and if she pushed him away, he would know that the damage he had done was irreparable.

The glow from the porch lit her face and she had never looked more beautiful. Larry reached his arm out to wrap around her and glanced at the house.

"I can't believe you did this. Is that where you were this morning?"

"I thought it was best if I stayed out of the way." Larry's breathing was shallow and labored from his heart hammering hard inside his chest. He was so afraid of rejection.

Jackie turned toward him and slipped her arms around his neck. "It's the best Christmas ever! I love it."

Relief flooded through him and Larry took a deep breath. Closing his eyes, he took in the scent of her hair as he tightened the embrace. "I'm sorry about all of our fights, all of my jealousy. I didn't want to come to terms with what I felt, and I didn't react well."

Jackie leaned back and looked up at Larry.

"I've missed you, Jackie."

"I've missed you, too." Jackie patted Larry's chest and looked again at her porch. "It's really beautiful. Thank you so much for the lights and the tree."

Larry shook his head. He wasn't handling this right. She didn't understand. "Jackie, I've missed us. I'm not me without you."

Jackie pulled away. "Now, Larry, nothing has really changed. I'm still going to be doing events, maybe even some out of town. You're still going to be working every night. We've tried this more than once and it always ends the same way."

"No, it's not the same. With my promotion, I'm working days now. I can go with you and help you with your events. I'm not the same now, Jackie. I know that I was not being fair to you. I was lashing out at you because I couldn't come to grips with the way I felt. I know all that now."

Jackie looked down and then leaned back against her car. He had managed his frustrations differently at his mother's house earlier, and he hadn't blamed her for Greg's flirtation. In the past he would have driven off and not spoken to her for days while he accused her of causing Greg's advances. There had been an improvement. "I don't know."

"Is it the city guy? Are you still working things out with him? I don't want to be your rebound guy. I want this to be for keeps."

"I think maybe Erik was the rebound guy," Jackie said turning into Larry's arms and looking up to accept his kiss.

Larry kissed her again, longer this time, hoping to convey how much he had suffered without her. "Well, if he brought you back to me, he did something right." Larry brushed the hair from Jackie's brow. "I'll pick you up in the morning. I want you to come to Mom's for Christmas day. It will be—"

"That's just for family, Larry. I've been there all day today and I shouldn't—"

Larry placed his index finger across her lips to silence her. "You are family, and I want us to go together as a couple."

Jackie felt that tingling burn in the back of her throat again as it tightened to hold back tears. "But your mom--"

"My mom will be ecstatic! She wished me good luck when I walked out tonight to follow you here. She's always told me that we were meant to be, and I needed to figure it out."

"She did tell me that she had that special gift, the gift of knowing what was right." Jackie recalled that awkward conversation they had a few weeks ago.

"And she's right," Larry said, stroking his thumb across her cheek. "You are my gift and I promise you I'll never forget that."

Jackie snuggled down into Larry's coat and closed her eyes tight. "Merry Christmas, Larry."

Larry smiled and held her close. "Merry Christmas, Jackie. I love you."

how many words do i need
to tell you i love you?
golden honey eyes
star filled skies
late night talks
long beach walks
whiskey and wishes
forbidden kisses
a million words
a million ways
all i need is
three

a. sparke

Follow a. sparke on Instagram @adeline.sparke

If you haven't read about Jackie's best
friend, Calinda Willow, you can find
her story in <u>Willow Wood</u>.

It's available in paperback, ebook, and
audio.

I'd love to hear from you!

You can find me on Facebook, Goodreads, Twitter, Instagram, or my website.

Sign up for my newsletter to learn about upcoming releases!

www.SheriRichey.com